CW00821016

everything is nice
and other fiction

everything is nice
and other fiction

Peter Owen
London and Chester Springs

PETER OWEN PUBLISHERS
73 Kenway Road, London SW5 0RE

Peter Owen book are distributed in the USA by
Dufour Editions Inc., Chester Springs, PA 19425-0007

First published in Great Britain 2001
Introduction © Peter Owen 2001; *Narcissus and Goldmund*
© Hermann Hesse 1957 (translation © Leila Vennewitz and Suhrkamp
Verlag 1992); 'Annunciation' © Anna Kavan 1958; 'The Delicate Prey'
© Paul Bowles 1949; 'Everything Is Nice' © Jane Bowles 1963;
The Ice Palace © Tarjei Vesaas 1963 (translation © Elizabeth Rokkan
and Peter Owen 1966, 1993); 'The House Boat' © Anaïs Nin 1948;
'The Bracelet' and 'The Victim' © Flammarion 1951, 1958 (translation
© Peter Owen 1971); 'Fag-End Blues' © Giulio Einaudi Editore 1960
(translation © A.E. Murch 1971); 'Despicable Bastard' © Shusaku Endo
1959 (translation © Van C. Gessel 1984); 'Alberta' and 'The Silken
Thread' © The Estate of Cora Sandel and Peter Owen 1986 (translation
© Elizabeth Rokkan and Peter Owen 1986); translation of 'Outside'
© Paul Bowles 1972; 'A Poet' © Fondo de Cultura Económica 1960
(translation © Octavio Paz and Eliot Weinberger 1976);
Chasing Black Rainbows © Jeremy Reed 1994; *Hermes in Paris*
© Peter Vansittart 2000; *Cassandra's Disk* © Angela Green 2001

All Rights Reserved. No part of this publication may be
reproduced in any form or by any means without the written
permission of the publishers.

ISBN 0 7206 1126 1

A catalogue record for this book is available from the British Library

Printed and bound in Great Britain by
MPG Books Ltd, Bodmin, Cornwall

Contents

List of illustrations

Independent Publishing
1951 to 2001

THE PUBLISHING FIRM of Peter Owen was started just six years after the end of the Second World War. Life was less frenetic in those days, certainly less mechanized. In Britain food was still rationed and foreign travel was subject to currency restrictions; £50 was the maximum that could be taken out of the country, though one could have a decent holiday abroad for that sum. I had just turned twenty-four, was single with some publishing experience, keen to work for myself and willing to work hard. I worked at home from my bedsit, an old typewriter my only equipment.

I had already gained some publishing experience with a number of the small firms that proliferated after the war and cashed in on the shortage of books. My first job was as an office boy at the Bodley Head, then a distinguished independent imprint owned by several leading publishers, the main shareholder being Stanley Unwin. When I left school I took a course in journalism, but after my efforts to break into this field began to seem unrealistic my father asked the assistance of my uncle, his brother-in-law Rudolph Friedman, who was working as manager of Zwemmers bookshop in Charing Cross Road. He took me to see Mr Unwin who employed me as a junior as a favour to one of his best customers. I was inexperienced and lazy and had very little idea of what a publisher actually did. Though I soon began enjoying the work, I realized that the Bodley Head was not going to give me any particularly useful skills or teach me enough to enable me to make a career in book publishing. I had decided that I liked the profession and that, even though I still saw it as the back door to journalism, it might make an fulfilling alternative. I subsequently worked for several other publishers, where I gained valuable experience, including learning what not to do.

During the war paper had been severely restricted and the quality was poor; publishers were given an allocation. In some ways this was no bad thing as publishers had to restrict themselves to publishing the more deserving books. Almost every title – unless there was something really wrong with it – sold out immediately. Prices were still cheap, though people did not appreciate this – British readers, having got used to public libraries, have always objected to paying a realistic price for books. After the war you could buy a novel for 7s. 6d ($37\frac{1}{2}$p) or a biography for between 10s. 6d and 12s. 6d ($52\frac{1}{2}$p and $62\frac{1}{2}$p).

In the late 1940s paper was still rationed, and as I had spent a short time in the Royal Air Force I was eligible for a Forces paper quota. This made me consider setting up a publishing company on my own – if I could raise the finance. When I was just twenty-one I met Neville Armstrong, who had a paper quota and also a little money. He had dabbled in publishing and wanted to launch a new imprint, so we started a company called Peter Nevill. We published good books, some recommended by my uncle, but the shortage of money meant that we had to look elsewhere, and another partner was brought in. Three was too many and we didn't get on, so I was bought out for a small sum. This – together with a bank overdraft of £350, guaranteed by my mother – was the basis of my capital, and it amounted to no more than £850. Even in 1951 this was a ludicrously small amount. A six-figure sum might have been a more realistic figure to launch a publishing house on a sound footing. However, I thought I would give it a try. It would not have mattered greatly if it had failed, as I had no commitments and few illusions. I could afford no staff, but I had acquired some experience, particularly in book production, which proved vital. I was lucky to have had excellent production training from, among others, Rudolph Ullstein, formerly a partner in the famous German firm Ullstein Verlag. My other asset was being able to type my own letters, which I did for the first two or three years.

Publishing then was much less risky than it is now. Britain had a well-funded public library system, and library orders assimilated part of every print run. Books were widely reviewed and if they received a good write-up libraries ordered several hundred copies within a few weeks. This made it much less of a gamble to publish new writers, and I was able to take chances. I found I could import small US editions of books, which meant less work producing the book and thus less capital outlay. It was possible to print 2,000 of almost any title, and it was likely that it would eventually sell out.

Soon the company was on a sound enough footing for it to expand. I had published two of Muriel Spark's books, *Emily Brontë* and *The Letters of John Henry Newman*, and she became my first editor. She left to further her full-time writing career, and my next editor was the novelist Elizabeth Berridge.

After the war my father and my uncle had started a small literary publishing house, Vision Press, and through them I had the contacts to appoint agents abroad. Exports then, particularly to British Commonwealth countries, accounted for around 40 per cent of turnover. Through my uncle I was introduced to James Laughlin of New Directions Books, one of the most distinguished American publishers, and he was very helpful to me in the early days. If we published the same title simultaneously, we would print both our editions together in the UK – thus reducing costs – and he would then import the larger American edition to the USA. Together we published Ezra Pound's *The Spirit of Romance*, Henry Miller's *Books in My Life*, an anthology of Russian literature – which included Boris Pasternak, who was then almost unknown in England – and Julien Gracq's novel *A Dark Stranger*. This was the nucleus of my first list.

Laughlin had been advised by Henry Miller that he should buy Hermann Hesse's novel *Siddhartha*, which Miller regarded as a masterpiece. Hesse at the time was almost unknown outside Germany, though he had been awarded the Nobel Prize for Literature in 1946, so I was able to buy *Siddhartha* with a £25 advance. It soon acquired a reputation, going into numerous hardback editions and becoming a cult book. Publishers fought for the paperback rights, which I refused to sell for a while, though when I eventually did the book became a major bestseller. In this volume I have included the first chapter of one of Hesse's other great novels, *Narcissus and Goldmund*, which we have since published in paperback in our Modern Classics series.

The prose selection in this anthology, which spans the fifty years, is all fiction and where possible I have included stories rather than extracts from novels.

Anna Kavan is only now achieving recognition as as one of the most remarkable authors of her time. She was always elegant in appearance, though a lifelong heroin addict. Since her death she has been compared to Virginia Woolf, Djuna Barnes and Anaïs Nin. She achieved some recognition as a writer under the name Helen Ferguson before the Second World War. She later changed her name to Anna Kavan, the name of the central character in her novel *Let Me Alone*. When I met her in the 1950s she was largely forgotten and had just paid for *A Scarcity of Love* – a title we have since reissued – to be published; the company concerned disappeared soon after the book came out. The first title of hers that we brought out was *Eagles' Nest*, which, though not one of her best books, is nevertheless highly distinctive. This was followed by a collection of brilliant stories called *A Bright Green Field*, one of which is included here. Since then we have published all her books. She died in 1968, not long after the publication of what many regard as her most important novel, *Ice*.

An author we introduced early on in translation to English-speaking readers was Cesare Pavese. The first book of his that we brought out was *Among Women Only*, and we have since published all of Pavese's significant writings in English. Pavese was one of the greatest twentieth-century Italian writers, and I have included a story typical of his style called 'Fag-End Blues'.

When we took on Anaïs Nin she was another author with an underground reputation; at the time she was little known in the UK or even in the USA, where she then lived. She had lived in Paris before the Second World War and was a close friend of Henry Miller, Lawrence Durrell and other now-famous authors. Apart from being a talented writer, she was very beautiful and was not shy of promoting herself – and she did it well. The first book I published was *Children of the Albatross*, though she is now better known for her *Journals* which, on account of their quality and the candid nature of the revelations contained in them, have become international bestsellers. After her death in 1977 and that of her husband Hugo Guyler – who used the pseudonym Ian Hugo – it became possible to publish her journals in an unexpurgated form. I have included the story 'Houseboat' from the collection *Under a Glass Bell*.

In the early 1960s I was on holiday in Morocco with my wife Wendy. Many years earlier I had read *The Sheltering Sky* by Paul Bowles and considered it brilliant. I discovered he was living in Tangier and, while we were there I obtained his address and contacted him. Paul was out when I called, but his wife, Jane, was at home with her servant Cherifa. Jane was very protective of Paul, but she arranged for us to come back the next day. He proved to be a very natural, modest man, an American expatriate with impeccable old-fashioned manners. His courtesy and genuine manner never wavered during the many years I knew him as a friend. On this first meeting he gave me a manuscript that he had just completed, a travel book entitled *Their Heads Are Green*. He said, 'You might wish to publish this' – and I did; it appeared in 1963. On our next visit to Morocco he gave me a collection of stories, most of which had never appeared in the UK, entitled *Pages from Cold Point*. Our edition was the first. One of those stories, 'The Delicate Prey', is included in this anthology.

On a subsequent visit he mentioned that Jane had had a book published in the 1940s when she was twenty-one, which had become a cult in the USA but which was little known elsewhere,

11

being long out of print. Copies of the book, *Two Serious Ladies*, were difficult to obtain, but I was told that Ruth Fainlight and her husband Alan Sillitoe were friends of the Bowleses and Jane had given Ruth her last copy. I persuaded Ruth to lend it to me; Wendy read the book first and raved about it. We realized it was a gem, and it was subsequently published by us to great acclaim. I suggested to Jane and Paul that I should handle Jane's foreign rights; they agreed and we sold the book in many countries. The novel was soon followed by a volume of stories, *Plain Pleasures*; one of these, 'Everything Is Nice', is included here. Her books remain in print all over the world.

Sadly Paul died aged eighty-nine in 1999, many years after Jane's death. I consider Paul one of the greatest English-language writers of the last century as well as a fine human being and friend.

In the late 1960s Elizabeth Rokkan, a distinguished British academic living in Norway, suggested that we publish Cora Sandel. She translated the superb *Alberta* trilogy and other Sandel books. The stories included here, 'Alberta' and 'The Silken Thread', are taken from the collection entitled *The Silken Thread*.

Elizabeth also translated The Ice Palace by Tarjei Vesaas. Vesaas was regarded as the most important contemporary Norwegian writer at the time but was little known outside his native country. Rather than writing in the heavily Danish-influenced Bokmål, the usual language of Norwegian literature, he wrote in Nynorsk, the hybrid 'New Norwegian' developed in the nineteenth century. I regard *The Ice Palace*, an extract of which is included here, as perhaps the best book we have ever published. Subsequently we produced translations of most of Vesaas's work. He was a modest man and an outstanding writer, a countryman who lived and died in the small village of Vinje in Telemark where he was born. His house is now a museum, and visitors still flock there. He was several times nominated for the Nobel Prize, but it is believed that it was not awarded to him for fear of accusations of nepotism. On one of his few visits to London, while he was over to promote the second novel that we published, *The Birds*, he was asked if he would like to receive the Nobel Prize. He thought for a moment and said, 'It would be a nuisance.' Perhaps luckily for him he was spared such recognition.

Another author that we first took on in the 1960s was Peter Vansittart, who is, in my opinion and that of many others, one of the most eminent yet underrated English writers. We have published fourteen of his novels and a few books of non-fiction, including his recent autobiography *Survival Tactics*. Peter has just turned eighty and is well overdue to receive the recognition his immense talent deserves. An extract from his latest novel, *Hermes in Paris*, which we published last year, is reproduced here.

One of the earlier books that the company brought out was a biography of Colette by Margaret Crosland, called Madame Colette. Colette was at that time being rediscovered, and some years later I was told that a number of her books were available to be published in England. I contacted her widower, Maurice Goudeket, and we subsequently published two novels – *Retreat from Love* and *Duo and Le Toutounier* – a volume of stories – *The Other Woman* – and several travel books and memoirs. Two of the stories from *The Other Woman*, 'The Bracelet' and 'Victim', are reprinted here. These were translated by Margaret Crosland, who has long been an admirer of Colette and who has advised on and been author or translator of many books on French art and literature that we have published. I am grateful for her expert advice over the years.

We introduced several Japanese books to English-speaking readers early in my career, including Yukio Mishima's brilliant *Confessions of a Mask*, so I developed an interest in Japanese literature. As a result I visited Japan and met Mishima and other writers, including Yasunari Kawabata, whom we also published. Soon after I discovered the Catholic novelist Shusaku Endo, who was then little known outside Japan. The first book of his that we published was *The Sea and Poison*, a brave book for a Japanese author to write, as it dealt with the vivisection of American prisoners of war in a Japanese hospital. I met Endo, liked him and, having read another of his novels, *Wonderful Fool*, realized what a great writer he was and resolved to continue publishing him. Perhaps his greatest novel is *Silence*, an account of the persecution of Japanese Christians and European missionaries who worked in Japan in the early seventeenth century. *Silence* is currently being filmed by US director Martin Scorsese. Many authors – including that other great Catholic writer Graham Greene – have considered Endo one of the greatest writers of the twentieth century, and we have published all his best books. Other than *Silence*, the most important novels are *The Samurai* and his last novel *Deep River*. Endo became a friend and appointed me as his international agent, and we ensured that his books were published all over the world. He was also a Nobel Prize candidate but, perhaps on account of his Catholicism and because many of his books were critical of Japanese society, he failed to receive the final Nobel nomination. In my opinion, this was a mistake, as Endo's books are accessible to all readers, regardless of their culture or faith. Endo was also the author of many fine stories, one of which – 'Despicable Bastard' from *Stained Glass Elegies* – is included in this collection.

In the late 1980s, just before he was awarded the Nobel Prize, we published two books by the Mexican poet Octavio Paz, *The Monkey Grammarian* and *Eagle or Sun*; a piece from the latter is in this volume. He had been nominated for the prize a number of times and was eventually honoured with the award. Paz was a modest man and always very pleasant to deal with. (Yet another Nobel Prize winner was the Guatemalan novelist Miguel Angel Asturias. The two books we issued by him, *The Cyclone* and *The Mulatta and Mr Fly*, helped him to get the prize, as some of the jury could not read his work in Spanish.)

There has been renewed interest in Isabelle Eberhardt over the past two decades, helped, no doubt, by Paul Bowles's selection from her work called *The Oblivion Seekers*, an extract of which is in this book. She was a trail-blazing woman, a pioneer of feminism, who lived and travelled in North Africa, often dressed as a man, at the end of the nineteenth century.

Coming up to date, we took on Jeremy Reed in the mid-1980s and have published a number of his books. I regard Jeremy as among the most talented and creative writers and poets of his generation, and he has received a number of prestigious poetry awards. Like most good writers he is ahead of his time. An extract from *Chasing Black Rainbows* – his novel based on the life of the Surrealist poet, dramatist and actor, Antonin Artaud – is included in this collection.

Angela Green's *Cassandra's Disk* is an exceptionally talented new novel. While we are always on the look-out for new writers, it is rare that ones finds a first novel of this quality and we agreed that it deserved to be published, despite the difficulties in marketing an unknown author.

In the fifty years I have worked in the industry publishing has changed almost beyond recognition: over the past twenty years or so the library system has been depleted through lack of funds and small bookshops have been replaced by large chains of stores. In some cases booksellers have become more efficient, especially since stock-control computerization, but sometimes there seems to be less personal enthusiasm in bookselling as well as in publishing. It has become more difficult to sell books, as the investment is much greater despite the advent of revolutionary new technology. An average print run for us is now 1,500 copies of a book, sometimes as few as 1,250. If we sell several thousand copies of a book in hardback this is an impressive sale for us as an independent publisher. It is much more difficult to publish new novelists and creative or experimental writing these days because of the high costs involved and the lack of reviewing space in the major newspapers for lesser-known writers.

The end of the Net Book Agreement has resulted in less shelf space for literary fiction and work in translation, as more is given over to discounted mainstream fiction. The traditional British export markets in the Commonwealth – in particular Canada,

Australia, New Zealand, India and South Africa – import far fewer books than they used to; domestic publishing has proliferated and these countries depend less and less on the UK to define their culture.

Fifty years ago relatively few books were published that originated in a foreign language; standards of translation were often poor and translators were paid pittances. Sales of such books were usually lower than that for books written in English. Many of my early books were translations of important but neglected European writers, such as Jean Cocteau, Jean Giono, Blaise Cendrars, Monique Wittig and Violette Leduc, whose autobiography, *La Bâtarde*, became an international bestseller in the 1960s. Translations are now more in evidence, and these are often of a very high standard. However, the expense of translating a book and the cost of editing the translator's work makes it is far more difficult to translate an unknown author, and publishers may require assistance from the originating country or from arts-funding bodies to make a work economically viable.

Sophisticated new technology has supplanted the manual typewriter and a number of traditional publishing and printing skills. This has cut costs in some areas, as many publishing companies now do most pre-press work in house. However, with the level of competition in the field of fiction, it is becoming increasingly hard to sell good literary fiction successfully, given the limited amount of bookshop space. When I started in the business, at least 50 per cent of our annual output consisted of fiction, but now now it is necessary to diversify and to publish a higher proportion of non-fiction titles, such as reference books and biographies. However, it is every publisher's ideal to introduce and publish talented new writers, and we intend to go on doing this as far as is possible, even in this difficult publishing climate.

More public money is required both for libraries and to help publishers, especially small independent publishers, to find new authors and promote them. Publishing is dominated by international conglomerates, who often neglect to publish the most original talent. If money is not forthcoming I foresee stagnation in terms of British publishing's literary and creative output.

I believe that as technology progresses the book will be replaced at least in part by electronic publishing. However, there will always be those who wish to hold and handle a book as an object, so that some will still continue to be produced. Design will no doubt improve as books become more expensive. Ones of significance published during the last century will become increasingly sought after by readers, and perhaps the fact that fewer books will be published in the future is in itself no bad thing, as most people would agree that too many are produced at the moment. Fewer books would make for a healthier market and enable publishers to sell more copies of those they decide to be worthy of publication.

This anthology contains some of the most important authors we have published over the years. I am grateful to these authors as I am to all my staff over the last fifty years, who are too numerous to name. However, I would single out for special thanks two of my longest-serving editors, who retired only relatively recently: Beatrice Musgrave and Michael Levien; they have made substantial contributions to the company. My daughter Antonia joined the firm four years ago as editorial director, thus ensuring continuity of editorial policy and guaranteeing the independent spirit of the company.

I hope readers will enjoy this selection – and that it may stimulate further reading!

Peter Owen

Grandfather by Marc Chagall, from his autobiography *My Life*

Hermann Hesse

HERMANN HESSE was born in Germany in 1877. The son and grandson of missionaries in India, Hesse ran away from theological school in Maulbronn. His first major success as a writer came with the novels *Peter Camenzind* (1904) and *Unterm Rad* (1905; translated as *The Prodigy*, 1957). These were followed by *Gertrud* (1910), *Rosshalde* (1914), *Demian* (1919) and *Siddhartha* (1922). After a visit to India in 1911, he settled in Switzerland, working for the Red Cross during the First World War. His later novels include *Der Steppenwolf* (1927), *Narziss und Goldmund* (1930) and *Das Glasperlenspiel* (1943; translated as *Magister Ludi*, 1950). His books were suppressed by the Nazis, but in 1946 he received world recognition with the Nobel Prize for Literature. He died in Switzerland in 1962.

'Hesse was a great writer in precisely the modern sense: complex, subtle, allusive; alive to the importance of play, to the desperate yet frolicsome game of writing.' – *New York Times Book Review*

Narcissus and Goldmund

This is the first chapter of Hesse's classic tale of flesh and the spirit. Narcissus is a teacher at a monastery in medieval Germany and Goldmund is his favourite pupil. While Narcissus remains detached from the world in prayer and meditation, Goldmund runs away in pursuit of love. From then on he lives a wanderer's life, his amatory adventures bringing both pain and ecstasy. His eventual reunion with Narcissus brings into focus the diversity between artist and thinker, Dionysian and Apollonian.

First issued by Peter Owen in 1957 as *Narziss and Goldmund*, this extract is taken from a new translation by Leila Vennewitz, published in 1994. One of Hesse's most enduring works, *Narcissus and Goldmund* has become a classic of contemporary literature.

AT THE MARIABRONN monastery entrance, with its rounded arch resting on double columns, stood a venerable Spanish chestnut tree, a solitary offspring of the south, brought back generations earlier by a pilgrim returning from Rome. Its broad, curving crown spread protectively across the path as it breathed in the wind, and in the spring, when everything around it had turned to green and even the monastery walnut trees were already showing their fresh, russet foliage, the chestnut's leaves were still taking their time. Then, when the nights were shortest, it would thrust up through the clusters of leaves the milky-green shafts of its exotic blossoms with their evocative, pungent scent. In the autumn wind of October, well after fruit and grapes had been harvested, its yellowing crown would shed the prickly crop that did not ripen every year, and the monastery boys would scuffle for the nuts that Subprior Gregor, himself a native of the south, would roast on the hearth in his room. Protective and exotic, the great tree gently waved its crown above the entrance to the monastery, a sensitive guest from a different, warmer climate, mysteriously related to the slender sandstone columns of the doorway and to the carved stonework of the window arches, sills and posts – beloved by southerners, gaped at as an alien by the locals.

Many generations of monastery pupils had passed below this alien tree, their slates tucked under their arms, chattering, laughing, playing, arguing; barefoot or shod, a flower between their lips or a nut between their teeth or a snowball in their hand, according to the season. New pupils kept coming; over the years the faces would change, but the boys tended to resemble each other, fair-skinned and curly haired. Some stayed on, became novices, then monks, had their heads shorn, wore cowl and rope, studied books, taught the boys, grew old, died. Others, their years of study completed, were taken home by their parents, to castles, to merchants' or artisans' houses, went out into the world to carry on their pastimes and trades, came back perhaps once to the monastery for a visit, now grown to manhood, bringing small sons to the monks as pupils, smiled as they gazed up at the chestnut tree, then dispersed again.

In the monastery cells and halls, among the heavy, rounded window arches and massive double columns of red stone, life went on with its teaching, studying, administering and governing. Many forms of art and science were practised here and handed down from one generation to the next – devout and secular, clear and obscure. Books were written and annotated, systems devised, ancient scriptures collected, manuscripts illuminated; the people's faith was nurtured, the people's faith smiled at. Scholarship and piety, naïveté and subtlety, wisdom of the Evangelists and wisdom of the Greeks, white magic and black. Some of all this flourished here; there was room for everything, as much room for isolation and penance as for conviviality and good living. Which of these became dominant depended on the personality of the abbot and on the prevailing trends of the day. At times the monastery was much sought out for its exorcists and demonologists, at others for its excellent music; at times for a saintly father who performed cures and miracles, at others for its fish soups and venison-liver pâtés, each in its own time. And always among the multitude of monks and pupils, the fervent and the lukewarm, the fasters and the fat, among the many who came, lived and died, there had always been the occasional individual, the outstanding one, who was loved by all or feared by all, one who seemed chosen, who continued to be talked about long after his contemporaries had been forgotten.

At this time the Mariabronn monastery also contained two outstanding individuals, an old man and a youth. Among the swarm of brothers filling the dormitories, chapels and study halls there were two whom all knew and respected. There was Abbot Daniel, the old man, and the pupil Narcissus, the youth, who had only recently entered the novitiate. Nevertheless, because of his exceptional gifts Narcissus had already, contrary to all tradition, been assigned to teaching, especially Greek. These two, the abbot and the novice, had a special standing in the monastery. They were watched and aroused curiosity; they were admired and envied as well as secretly derided.

The abbot was loved by almost everyone. Full of goodness, simplicity and humility, he had no enemies. Only the scholars of the monastery tempered their affection with a little condescension, for while Abbot Daniel may have been a saint, a scholar he was not. He possessed the simplicity that is wisdom, but his Latin was modest, his Greek non-existent.

Those few who occasionally smiled at the abbot's simplicity were all the more enchanted by Narcissus, the wonder boy, the handsome youth with such elegant Greek, with the faultless aristocratic bearing, the quiet, penetrating thinker's gaze and the narrow, finely chiselled lips. The scholars loved him for his wonderful Greek. Almost everyone loved him for his nobility and refinement; many fell in love with him. Some resented his extreme quietness and self-control, his courtly manners.

Abbot and novice: each in his own way bore the fate of the chosen; dominating in his own way, suffering in his own way. Each felt more akin to the other, more attracted to him, than to the rest of the monastic community. Yet neither could get close to the other; neither could warm to the other. The abbot treated the youth with the utmost care, the utmost consideration, was concerned for him as for a rare, delicate, perhaps precocious, perhaps endangered, brother. The youth accepted every order, every advice, every word of praise from the abbot with perfect composure, never contradicting, never put out; and if the abbot's assessment of him was correct and his only vice was pride, he was wonderfully skilful at concealing it. There was nothing that could be said against him; he was perfect, superior to everyone. Yet few, apart from the scholars, really became friends with him, and his superiority enveloped him like a chilling cloud.

'Narcissus,' the abbot said one day after hearing his confession, 'I must admit to being guilty of having judged you harshly. I have often considered you proud, and I may have done you an injustice. You are very much alone, my young brother. You are lonely, you have admirers but no friends. I wish I had cause to rebuke you now and again, but I never have reason to do so. I wish you would sometimes misbehave, the way most young people of your age so readily do. You never do. There are times when I am a little anxious about you, Narcissus.'

The youth raised his dark eyes to the old man.

'I greatly desire, gracious Father, not to cause you any anxiety. It may well be that I am proud, gracious Father. I ask you to punish me for that. At times I even wish to punish myself. Send me to a hermitage, Father, or order me to perform lowly duties.'

'For both those things you are too young, dear brother,' said the abbot. 'Moreover, you have a great capacity for languages and thinking, my son. It would be a waste of those gifts from God if I were to assign you to lowly duties. Probably you will become a teacher and a scholar. Do you not wish that yourself?'

'Forgive me, Father, I am really not so sure about my wishes. I shall always take pleasure in scholarly pursuits – how could I do otherwise? But I do not believe that those will be my only sphere. After all, it may not always be a person's wishes that determine his destiny and mission. It may be something else, something predestined.'

The abbot listened gravely, yet there was a smile on his old face as he said: 'From whatever knowledge I have acquired about human beings, it seems we all tend, especially in our youth, to confuse providence with our wishes. But since you believe you have some foreknowledge of your destiny, tell me something about it. For what do you believe yourself destined?'

Narcissus half closed his dark eyes so that they disappeared under his long black lashes. He said nothing.

'Speak, my son,' the abbot prompted him after a long wait.

In a low voice and with downcast eyes, Narcissus began to speak: 'I believe I know, gracious Father, that above all I am destined for the monastic life. I shall, I believe, become a monk, a priest, a subprior and perhaps an abbot. I do not believe this because I wish it. My wish is not to hold office, but offices will be imposed upon me.'

For a long time neither spoke.

'Why do you believe this?' the old man asked hesitatingly. 'What can there be in your character, apart from your erudition, that finds expression in that belief?'

'It is the attribute,' Narcissus said slowly, 'of having a feeling for the nature and destiny of people, not only for my own but for those of others, too. This attribute compels me to serve others by having power over them. Had I not been born to the monastic life I would have to become a judge or a statesman.'

'That may be,' the abbot nodded. 'Have you tested your ability to recognize people and their destinies on any examples?'

'I have.'

'Are you prepared to give me an example?'

'I am.'

'Good. Since I would not like to pry into the secrets of our brothers without their knowledge, perhaps you would care to tell me what you believe you know about me, your abbot Daniel.'

Narcissus raised his lids and looked the abbot in the eye.

'Is that an order, gracious Father?'

'An order.'

'I find it difficult to speak, Father.'

'I, too, find it difficult, my young brother, to compel you to speak. Yet I do so. Speak!'

Narcissus bent his head and continued in a whisper: 'There is not much that I know about you, reverend Father. I know that you are a servant of God who would rather be a goatherd, or ring a little bell in a hermitage and take confessions from the peasants, than rule over a great monastery. I know that you have a special love for the holy Mother of God and pray most often to Her. Sometimes you pray that Greek and other knowledge pursued in this monastery may not confuse or endanger the souls of those in your charge. Sometimes you pray that you may not lose patience with Subprior Gregor. Sometimes you pray for a peaceful end. And your prayers will, I believe, be heard, and you will have a peaceful end.'

There was silence in the abbot's little reception room. At last the old man spoke. 'You are a visionary,' the aged abbot said with a smile. 'Even pious and kindly visions can deceive. Do not rely upon them, even as I do not. Can you see into my heart, Brother Visionary, and know what I am thinking about this matter?'

'I can see, Father, that you are thinking most kindly about it. You are thinking as follows: "This young pupil is in some slight danger. He has visions, he may have meditated overmuch. I could impose a penance on him. It would do him no harm. But I shall also take upon myself the penance I impose upon him." That is what you have just been thinking.'

The abbot rose. With a smile he indicated to the novice that it was time for him to leave. 'Very well,' he said. 'Do not take your visions too seriously, my young brother. God requires many things from us other than having visions. Let us assume that you have flattered an old man by promising him an easy death. Let us assume that for a moment the old man was glad to hear this promise. Now it is enough. You are to pray a rosary, tomorrow after early mass. You are to pray with humility and devotion and not perfunctorily, and I shall do the same. Now go, Narcissus, we have talked enough.'

On another occasion Abbot Daniel had to mediate between the youngest of the teaching monks and Narcissus, who could not agree on a certain point in the curriculum. Narcissus argued passionately for the introduction of certain changes in the teaching methods and was able to justify these convincingly. Father Lorenz, on the other hand, out of a kind of jealousy, refused to consider them, and each new discussion was followed by days of hurt silence and sulking, until Narcissus, convinced that he was right, would bring up the subject again. Finally Father Lorenz said, in a slightly offended tone: 'Very well, Narcissus, let us put an end to this argument. You know that it is for me to decide, not you. You are not my colleague but my assistant, and it is for you to yield to me. However, since the matter seems to be of such great importance to you, and since, though superior to you in authority, I am not your superior in knowledge and talent, I shall not make the decision myself. Instead we shall put it before our Father Abbot and let him decide.'

This they did, and Abbot Daniel listened patiently and benignly to the two scholars' argument about their views on teaching grammar. After they had both presented and backed up their opinions at length, the abbot looked at them with a twinkle, shook his old grey head a little, and said:

'Dear brothers, I am sure neither of you believes that I know as much about these matters as you do. It is laudable of Narcissus that he should have the school so much at heart, and that he should be trying to improve the curriculum. But if his superior is of a different opinion, Narcissus must be silent and obey, for no amount of improvement in the school could be set above any disruption of the order and obedience in this house that would result. I must rebuke Narcissus for not knowing when to yield. And as for you two young scholars, I wish you may never lack for superiors who are more stupid than you! There is no better remedy for pride.'

With this good-natured little joke he dismissed them. But he was careful to keep an eye on them during the next few days to see whether the two young teachers were once again on good terms.

And now it came about that a new face appeared in the monastery which saw so many faces come and go, and that this new face was not among the unnoticed and fast forgotten. It was a youth who, already enrolled in advance by his father, arrived one spring day to become a pupil at the monastery school. They, the youth and his father, tethered their horses to the chestnut tree and were met by the doorkeeper emerging from the entrance.

The boy looked up at the still leafless tree. 'I have never seen a tree like that,' he said. 'What a strange, beautiful tree! I wish I knew what it was called!'

The father, an elderly gentleman with a careworn, somewhat pinched face, ignored the boy's words, but the doorkeeper, who immediately took a liking to the boy, told him the name of the tree. The boy thanked him politely, held out his hand, and said: 'My name is Goldmund, and I am to go to school here.' The man gave him a smile and led the new arrivals through the entrance and up the wide stone staircase. Thus Goldmund entered the monastery with confidence and the feeling of having already met two beings in this place whose friend he could be: the tree and the doorkeeper.

The new arrivals were received first by Father Principal, then in the evening by the abbot himself. On both occasions the father, an imperial official, presented his son Goldmund; and although he was invited to remain in the house for a while as a guest, he made use of his right to hospitality for only one night, stating that he would have to return home the next day. As a gift he offered the monastery one of his two horses, and the gift was accepted. The conversation with the two clerics was polite and cool, but both the abbot and the principal looked upon the respectfully silent Goldmund with favour. They immediately liked the handsome boy with the delicate features. As for the father, they felt no regret at his departure the following day, whereas they were glad to keep the son.

Goldmund was introduced to the teachers and assigned a bed in the pupils' dormitory. Respectfully and with a sad expression he said goodbye to his father as the latter rode away, gazing after him until he disappeared between granary and mill through the narrow arched gate of the outer courtyard. A tear hung from one fair eyelash when the boy turned round, but the doorkeeper was already at hand to welcome him with an affectionate pat on the shoulder.

'Young master,' he consoled him, 'you mustn't be sad. At first most of the boys feel a bit homesick for their father and mother or their brothers and sisters. But you'll soon find out – life's quite good here too, in fact not bad at all.'

'Thank you, Brother Doorkeeper,' the boy replied. 'I have no brothers or sisters, and no mother. I have only my father.'

'Well then, you'll find friends instead, and scholarship and music and new games you've never heard of, all kinds of things, you'll see. And if you need a helping hand at any time, just come to me.'

Goldmund smiled at him. 'Oh, thank you so much! And if you want to do me a favour, please show me some time where our horse is kept, the one my father left here. I'd like to go and see it and make sure it's being looked after.'

The doorkeeper took him along at once and led him into the stable next to the granary. In the dim light there was a sharp smell of horses, of manure and barley, and in one of the stalls Goldmund found the brown horse that had carried him there. The animal had already recognized him and stretched out its head towards him. Goldmund placed his two hands around its neck, leaned his cheek against the broad forehead with the white patch, stroked the animal fondly and whispered into its ear: 'How are you, Blaze, dear pony, good boy, are you all right? Do you still love me? Have they fed you? Are you homesick too? Dear Blaze, dear little fellow, how glad I am you're staying here too. I'll come and visit you often and make sure you're all right.' From his cuff he pulled a piece of bread he had saved from breakfast and fed it in little pieces to the animal. Then he said goodbye and followed the doorkeeper across the courtyard, which was as wide as the market square of a big town and had linden trees growing here and there on it. At the inner entrance he thanked the doorkeeper, but after shaking hands with him realized he had forgotten the way to his classroom, which he had been shown the previous day. He gave a little laugh, blushed and asked the doorkeeper to show it to him, which he gladly did. In the classroom Goldmund found a dozen boys and youths seated on benches, and Narcissus, the teaching assistant, turned round.

'I am Goldmund,' he said, 'the new pupil.'

Narcissus nodded briefly. Without smiling, he indicated a place on a bench at the back and at once resumed the lesson.

Goldmund sat down. He was amazed to find such a young teacher, scarcely a few years older than himself – amazed and pleased to find this young teacher so handsome, so distinguished-looking, so serious, yet so attractive and charming. The door-keeper had been kind, the abbot had given him a friendly welcome; over in the stable stood Blaze, a little bit of home, and now here was this amazingly young teacher, with the gravity of a scholar and the nobility of a prince, and with such a disciplined, cool, compelling voice! He listened gratefully, yet without imme-diately grasping the nature of the subject. He felt at ease. He had landed among good, worthy people, and he was prepared to love them and to seek their friendship. As he lay in bed after waking up that morning, still tired from the long journey, he had felt appre-hensive, and in saying goodbye to his father he had been unable to hold back a few tears. But now everything seemed all right: he was content. Gazing long and often at the young teacher, he delighted in the firm, slender figure, the coolly flashing eyes, the firm lips forming clear, crisp syllables, the vibrant, untiring voice.

But when the lesson was over and the pupils scrambled noisily to their feet, Goldmund was startled and somewhat ashamed to realize that he had been asleep for quite a while. Nor was he the only one to notice: the other boys on his bench had noticed too and had passed along the information in whispers. The young teacher was scarcely out of the room before the other boys started tugging and cuffing Goldmund from all sides.

'Had a good sleep?' one of them asked with a grin.

'Fine pupil!' mocked another. 'Sure to become a great luminary of the Church! Nods off in the very first lesson!'

'Take the little brat to bed!' someone suggested, and amid general laughter they seized him by the arms and legs to carry him off.

Furious at being roused in this way, Goldmund hit out in all directions, trying to get free, and was cuffed and finally dropped while one of them still hung on to his foot. He violently kicked him away, hurled himself at the nearest boy who didn't back off, and was immediately involved in a fierce fight. His opponent was a hefty fellow, and the rest of them watched the contest gleefully. When Goldmund did not succumb and landed a few good punches on his hefty adversary, he quickly gained some friends among the others even without knowing the name of a single one of them. But suddenly they all scattered in haste, seconds before Father Martin, the school principal, entered and stood before the sole remaining boy. In some surprise he stared at Goldmund, whose blue eyes looked with embarrassment out of his beet-red, somewhat battered face.

'Well, well, what's the matter with you?' he asked. 'You're Goldmund, aren't you? Did they do you any harm, those young ruffians?'

'Oh no,' said the boy. 'I took care of him!'

'Took care of whom?'

'I don't know. I don't know any of them yet. One of them fought me.'

'I see. Did he start it?'

'I don't know. No, I think I started it myself. They were teasing me, and I got angry.'

'Well, you're off to a fine start, my boy. Now remember this. If you ever get into another fight here in the schoolroom, you'll be punished. And now hurry up and go to supper – off you go!'

Smiling, he watched the contrite Goldmund running off and trying as he ran to comb his ruffled fair hair with his fingers.

Goldmund was himself of the opinion that his first deed in this monastic life had been pretty stupid and naughty. Somewhat remorseful, he went in search of his schoolmates and found them at supper, but he was welcomed with friendly respect. He made honourable peace with his enemy and from then on felt accepted by the group.

Self-portrait by Anna Kavan

Anna Kavan

ANNA KAVAN, née Helen Woods, was an enigma, both in her life and her writing. She was born in Cannes – probably in 1901; she was, at best, evasive about the facts of her life – and spent her childhood in Europe, the USA and England. Her life was haunted by a rich, glamorous mother, beside whom her father remains an indistinct figure. Twice married and divorced, she began writing while living with her first husband in Burma and was initially published under her married name of Helen Ferguson. These early books were somewhat eccentric 'Home Counties' novels, but everything changed after her second marriage collapsed. In the wake of this, she suffered the first of many nervous breakdowns and was confined to a clinic in Switzerland. She emerged from her incarceration with a new name – Anna Kavan, the protagonist of her 1930 novel *Let Me Alone* – an outwardly different persona and a new literary style. She suffered periodic bouts of mental illness and long-term drug addiction – she had become addicted to heroin in the 1920s and continued to use it for the rest of her life – and these facets of her life feature prominently in her work. She destroyed almost all of her personal correspondence and most of her diaries, therefore ensuring that she achieved her ambition to become one of 'the world's best-kept secrets'. She died in 1968 of heart failure, soon after the publication of her most celebrated work, the novel *Ice*.

'One of the most mysterious of modern writers, Anna Kavan created a uniquely fascinating fictional world. Faithful to her obsessions, she pursued her dreams of ice and heroin to the end. Few contemporary novelists could match the fierce intensity of her vision.' – J.G. Ballard

Annunciation

This story is taken from the collection *A Bright Green Field*, first published by Peter Owen in 1958.

EVEN BEFORE SHE was awake Mary knew something had happened. All night long some frightening thing had slid in and out of her dreams, like the hawk which sometimes came gliding over the pigeon-house, planing off on a single wing-beat, only to float back a few minutes later, silent and inescapable as its own shadow.

Her last dream had been the bad water dream. The dream of water slowly filling the house, climbing stair after stair, creeping along the passages, under her door, filling her room till it lapped the bed and touched her with many cold mouths, sucking her fingertips and the lobes of her ears. The danger of this dream was that she might scream. And if she screamed Edith would stride in like a giantess, shaking the floor, making the tooth-glass chatter upon the shelf.

'Nightmares again?' Edith would say, snatching up the mosquito net and peering at her. When Edith was cross her eyes vanished in the folds of her face which looked heavy and pale and moist as the crumb of a loaf. 'Her ladyship won't like to hear that. She *will* be put out.'

'I didn't scream. I didn't scream,' Mary kept telling herself as she came awake.

There was no time for relief. She knew immediately that something had happened far worse than a scream, an unspeakable thing, she couldn't tell what it was. She only knew that it made her think of an appalling event which had taken place years ago, when she was still just a tiny girl, too little to dress herself. It was the most terrible thing in her whole life. Even thinking about it now made her press her face into the pillow. She tried to hide the memory under the pillow, but out it came; she would never forget the shock of waking up in the midnight room, all the familiar things with changed midnight faces. All over again now she felt the shock of being pulled out of bed, the harsh touch of clean things as cold as ice, the scolding, angry voices, her own tears which seemed as if they would never stop. The greatest shock of all had been the sight of her grandmother standing there in her room, tall and strange in a dressing-gown embroidered with peacocks' tails, saying that Mary wasn't a baby now, she ought to be ashamed of being a dirty girl. 'Disgusting!' Grandmother had said, and all the eyes in the peacocks' tails had flashed furiously. Even now Mary could have cried to think of Grandmother walking through the mysterious nightbound house, all on her account, to her everlasting shame.

'But that was ages ago. Nothing like that could happen now. I couldn't *possibly*.' So Mary tried to convince herself, although deep within her she already knew. She lifted the sheet to make certain. At once her heart started jumping about in her chest.

'Oh God, what shall I do?' The light from the open window was like God's eye, much too bright to bear. The spider's web meshes of the mosquito net had caught her with her shame. 'Oh God, let it not have happened. Oh God,' she prayed, 'please take it away.'

But when she peeped under the sheet again it was there.

Mary felt hot and sticky inside her nightdress. Her heart made more noise than the garden boys raking the gravel under her window. 'Be sure you never let the native boys catch sight of you,' Grandmother had told her with the solemn face reserved for important things. 'Never go near the window until you're dressed.' But the window was high, all Mary could see, looking out, was the pigeon-cote in the sky.

She jumped up, thrust the mosquito net on one side, and ran to the wash-basin. With her wet sponge she scrubbed and scrubbed at the sheet. The mark got fainter, its edges became blurred, but disappear it would not. She was in despair. 'I must get it into the basin and wash it with soap.'

In a sort of frenzy she tugged at the bottom sheet which the well-tucked-in blanket persisted in holding fast. 'Hurry! Hurry, before Edith comes!' Mary was shaking, her thin arms, pale as candles, seemed to have no strength in them at all.

'And what, miss, do you think you're doing, if one may ask?'

Mary had not heard Edith come in. A whimper she couldn't keep back escaped from behind the hand pressed to her mouth at that grim, questioning voice. She turned round and faced the big woman with swimming eyes, a midget in front of a giantess.

'Oh, Edith, I couldn't help it. It's not my fault. I don't know what happened,' she blurted out, frightened and full of guilt.

The maid took one look.

'Get back to bed and stay there till I come. I'll have to tell her ladyship about this.'

Out marched Edith like a dragoon; the tooth-glass quaked an accompaniment to her steps.

Mary did as she had been told. No matter how she curled herself up she could not avoid the wet patch her sponge had made, the clammy sheet was unpleasant to lie upon: it didn't occur to her to disobey, or even to lie outside the bedclothes. Except that every now and then she shivered, she lay quite still, her arms straight down beside her. One or two tears crossed her pale cheeks and found their way unnoticed into her hair.

Edith went pounding through the big house with a righteous tread. A native servant polishing the floor of the long gallery stood aside meekly while the white maid strode past him without a glance.

Plain and functional in her starched dress, massively planted on thick ankles and flat-heeled shoes, Edith stood at attention in the delicate room where her mistress sat up in bed, drinking coffee out of a Dresden cup. Her ladyship did not look old enough to be a grandmother. Her hair was beautifully waved and tinted, her face pink and unlined. Sitting there in a little lace jacket, she looked almost girlishly sweet.

But as she listened to Edith's message her expression grew hard.

'Are you sure? It seems impossible at her age – so young. What is she, ten or eleven? I thought we had another three years at least before this problem cropped up.'

'I've heard that with – with people like Miss Mary, it starts sooner.' The maid was deferential but privileged. Years of intimate service entitled her to a specialized intimacy.

'Most unfortunate. Most provoking,' her ladyship said, with a frown. 'Well, we must think what to do for the best. Oh dear, what an affliction.' She put the coffee cup down with a little clash and pushed aside the bed table which worked on a movable arm. Her breakfast was spoiled. She did not want to finish the coffee or eat the dainty triangles of toast in the silver rack. 'Take it away,' she said petulantly.

Edith picked up the tray and stood stolidly holding it in her hands. She knew there was more to come. She had been with her mistress so long that she could practically read her thoughts. 'She's a clever one, she is,' she said to herself, waiting, discreetly silent. She knew that the brain behind the tinted waves set by her hand was busily seeking the angle which would suit her best, surveying the situation from all sides, twisting it this way and that, as if she were trying on a new hat.

At length the pronouncement came. 'We must take every precaution. With all these natives about you never know. We can't risk a catastrophe. From now on Mary must never go out alone. In fact, I think she had better not leave the grounds. The fewer people she sees the better, for all our sakes. Now that she's getting older, people are beginning to notice that she's not very bright – not quite like other children of her age. Once or twice lately I've felt quite embarrassed. Perhaps it's just as well this has happened, so that she has to be kept out of the way. Yes, perhaps it's a blessing in disguise.'

The mistress and the maid exchanged understanding looks. They really understood one another extremely well.

'I'll have to talk to her. You can get my bath ready, Edith,' the grandmother said.

She was silent while her hair was being done. On her reflected face in the glass Edith saw the look, bitter, angry and sad, which meant she was thinking about her daughter.

'I wonder if Mary can have inherited any characteristics?' There were no secrets between the two women. 'Have you noticed her talking to men? I have an idea that James –'

'He's fond of children. I dare say she does hang round the garage at times.' The maid took a hairpin out of her mouth and transfixed a curl.

'There you are! It's showing itself already. I must speak to James. You don't think he gives her any encouragement?'

Edith shook her head as vigorously as she could with her mouth full of hairpins. 'No, I don't.' The chauffeur hadn't been on the staff long, and she had no intention of seeing him go yet awhile. Handsome young white drivers were scarce. He wasn't going to get into disfavour if she could help it. 'James knows his place,' she said emphatically. 'He wouldn't stand for any monkey business, I know.'

'I'm glad to hear it,' her ladyship said. 'All the same, we can't be too careful,' she added, with a deep sigh.

'You're to stop here in your room till her ladyship comes. She wants to speak to you,' Edith told Mary, when she had finished with her. Then she stumped off and left her alone.

Mary waited. She waited so long that her frightened feeling almost went away. It didn't quite go, because, since Edith had been in, it was impossible for Mary to forget that something quite extraordinary had happened to her thin body which so often felt queer and tired. Edith hadn't spoken in her angry voice to make Mary feel wicked, but in the impatient voice she used when Mary was ill, to make her feel she was a nuisance. She was glad when Edith went out of the room. It seemed to Mary that whenever she was with anybody she spent her time trying not to make the person angry or to give them trouble. But it was no use. She always did one or the other. It was better to be alone. She wished Grandmother wasn't coming to talk to her. But at once, with a guilty start, she drove that wish away.

Now that she was dressed she could go to the window. Because it was so high, she could only see, while she stood on the floor, the blue sky, the pigeon-cote abandoned by pigeons during the heat of the day, and lower down a bit of the garage roof. If she climbed on to the window-sill, she could see the gravel sweep and the whole of the garage, the dog kennels, and some of the drive with trees on each side. She scrambled up, feeling guilty again. She had never been expressly forbidden to do this, because no one had ever caught her on the window-sill, but she knew instinctively that it would be forbidden. She glanced back into the room, listening for footsteps in the passage.

Everything was quiet, so she leaned her forehead against the mosquito screen and looked out. The gravel was still in immaculate ripples as it had been left by the rakes of the garden boys; no car had disturbed it so far. On the grass plot round the pigeon-house, the white pigeons lay in tormented shapes, gasping with heat, like things broken upon the rack, their wings partly stretched. The Alsatians were not to be seen. Chained in their kennels, they were sleeping off the rigours of their night watch. The blazing sunshine lay on everything like a brand.

Presently, from the black shadow inside the garage, a man appeared. His white shirt, rolled well above the elbows and open over the chest, was dazzling as he sauntered out, carrying something carefully in both hands. Mary watched breathless as he approached, strolling with the sun strong on his young brown neck, his brown head bare to the sun.

'James! James!' she called, in a queer little mouse-like cry, scratching mouse-like on the mosquito wire.

He stood on the grass plot. The shadow of the pigeon-house pole cut past him, a straight black blade. He raised his young, tough, handsome face to the window, and winked.

'What is it, James? What have you got there?' Mary pressed her cheek so hard on the wire that it burned her skin, but she didn't notice.

'A youngster.' He opened his hands, lifting them, cupped, so that she saw the small white feathered softness palpitating on his big palms. 'It fell out last night and I put it back. But I must have put it into the wrong nest, because this morning it was down again, pretty well pecked apart. They do that, pigeons, to a young one that isn't theirs. Now I've fixed it up and I'm going to have another shot at putting it back where it belongs.' He stood on tiptoe on the grass, and his upstretched arms were just long enough to reach the shelf running round the cote. He put the young pigeon down carefully, edging it with his fingers towards one of the holes.

Looking down from above, Mary saw the bird struggling in a senseless panic, its immature feathers awry, while the brown fingers, acting sightlessly, cleverly, by themselves, urged it into the nest. There was a final wild flurry before it vanished inside.

'There. We shan't know if it's in the right place till the other birds come back later.' Brushing his hands against each other, the chauffeur stepped back and looked up at Mary again. 'Keep your eyes open, and if they throw the poor bastard out, let me know. Not that it'll be much good. They'll finish it off next time. Proper devils they are, pigeons.'

The young man winked a second time, turned, and strolled off negligently with his short shadow. The gravel crunched rhythmically under his feet, his shoulders swayed in the barest suggestion of a dance rhythm. He didn't look back.

Mary watched till the garage entrance engulfed him. Then she slipped down from the window-sill just in time; someone was opening her door.

'Why, Mary, how queer you look! One side of your face is all red.'

Grandmother came crisply across the room, pattering on her high white heels. She was wearing a dress with roses on a pale ground; a beautiful dress that made her look like one of the china figures downstairs which mustn't be touched. As usual, she looked almost frighteningly fresh and cool, too perfect to touch, like the figures. She put her cool ringed fingers on Mary's cheeks where the wire had been pressing.

'How hot you are, child. Are you feverish, I wonder? You ought to have stayed in bed. Come, lie down, and I'll sit beside you.'

Mary got on to the bed obediently, first taking off her slippers as she had been taught. She felt guilty because she had been on the window-sill. Half expecting Grandmother to know what she had done, she darted a nervous sidelong glance. But the rose dress was only disposing itself in the chair by the bed, fanning out in graceful folds.

'Now, Mary, I've got something rather unpleasant to say; something that's not nice to talk about. You must listen carefully like a sensible girl and be sure you understand me. Then we won't ever speak of it again.'

What was coming next? What was Grandmother going to say? Her face was solemn and set as if she were angry. But she couldn't be angry because she took Mary's hand. Her fingers, however, felt angry. They closed firm and cool round Mary's hot hand and held it tight. The rings bit into her skin as if a trap had snapped shut. Mary felt confused by the kind gesture which had no feeling of kindness. Her grandmother's hand was soft and white; how could it feel like a trap? Fright crept into her confusion, she wanted to pull her hand away, it twitched, and the hard fingers tightened round it.

'Do you understand, Mary? Are you listening to me?'

'Oh yes, Grandmother,' she cried, praying Grandmother wouldn't know that this wasn't the truth. She tried desperately hard to attend to the words about growing up and becoming a woman and what a woman should know. But all the time she was confused by the strangeness of lying down in the daytime with Grandmother holding her hand and refusing to let it go. The diamond teeth glittered: if only they wouldn't bite her hand she could listen much better.

'But what's it mean? What's it to do with me?' Suddenly she was in a panic, just like the pigeon when it was put on the shelf. 'I am a little girl!' Over and over again she'd been told so. 'Little girls must do this. Little girls can't do that.' How could she suddenly be a woman as well? Her hand twitched more violently now. For the life of her she couldn't keep it still.

'Don't fidget so!'

Her hand was deposited on the counterpane with something between a pat and a slap. She started to rub it with the other hand, but remembered not to in time. She was glad to have her hand to herself again. She felt less afraid. Quickly she answered, 'Yes,' when Grandmother asked if she remembered seeing Mona the other day. Of course she remembered. She almost smiled, remembering Mona's big black smiling face and purple bandanna.

'Mona's going to have a baby. That's why she's got so big. That's what happens to women if they aren't careful. It might happen to you.'

Mary turned her head sharply, frightened again. The words meant nothing much, but the voice frightened her, it was so altered. Everything seemed to be changing, as if she were in a bad dream.

'Why this should be inflicted upon us at your age I don't know. Most girls are much older before it happens – white girls, anyhow. It's like a nigger – disgusting.'

Grandmother got up suddenly and started walking about the room. Her voice, her face, everything about her, was different and frightening. She wasn't herself at all. And she had said it again: the shameful, unforgettable word had again been spoken.

The room seemed to swell and contract through the tears in Mary's eyes.

'Not that it's your fault. I'm not blaming you. There's nothing to cry about,' Grandmother said.

But now that Mary had begun crying she could not stop. The tears simply rolled independently out of her eyes. She groped in her pocket and tugged her handkerchief out. But as fast as she wiped the tears away others came. Through a wavering mist she saw the rose patterned dress coming near. She blinked to get rid of her tears, and the centres of the roses blinked back at her fiercely, like peacocks' eyes.

'Pull yourself together now, Mary dear. There's no need for all this fuss.'

She heard the kind-not-kind voice in dismay. 'If she holds my hand again I shall scream. I shan't be able to help it,' she thought. And the thought shocked her, she had no idea there was so much wickedness in her. Grandmother only patted her shoulder.

'Don't cry. I'm going to take care of you. As long as you're a good girl and do as I tell you you'll be all right. I shall protect you from everything. It's a duty I owe your poor mother. If only I'd been stricter with her she wouldn't have married your father and you – and all this wouldn't have happened.'

The eyes withdrew. Grandmother was again walking about the room. She stopped at the foot of the bed.

'You must promise me something, Mary. It's very serious. I want you to promise faithfully never to speak to anyone unless I'm with you, or to go out except with Edith or me. You see, dear, you're not quite like other girls. And men are such beasts. Some man might take advantage – Perhaps you've wondered why I've not sent you to school or let you have friends of your own age. It's for your own sake, dear, because I don't want you to suffer. You've never been away from this house, where everyone is so kind to you and loves you. You've no idea how cruel the world can be. You can't imagine how people would hurt you. So that's why you must promise not to speak to anybody. If I find you've been talking to James I shall dismiss him at once.'

Mary's thoughts seemed to be playing leapfrog inside her head. No sooner did she try to catch one than it rushed away, leaving a different idea in its place. Now it was the young pigeon she seemed to see, flapping in senseless terror, its pink skin showing between its dishevelled plumes.

'Give me your word. Say "I promise."'

'I promise,' she said.

'There's my good girl!' Grandmother was suddenly smiling, putting a sort of lovingness into her voice. 'Isn't it lucky you've got me to take care of you and understand you so well? And this lovely house and garden to live in – no need ever to go outside. Perhaps we'll give you another room, nicer even than this one, on the other side where you'll see nothing but flowers. How would you like to have the room looking over the lily pool?'

'I like to see the pigeons,' said Mary. But Grandmother seemed not to hear.

'Stand up,' she said, 'and let me look at my big girl.' She took Mary's hand and helped her off the bed.

'My shoes!' Mary protested. Didn't Grandmother see she was in her stockinged feet? She let herself be steered across to the long mirror. Grandmother touched her chest.

'This dress – it's getting too tight already. We must get you a new one at once. And brassieres, too. I'll tell Edith to see to it. You must make yourself look at flat as possible so that people won't notice you're different from other girls of your age. We must do our best to hide it.'

If only this horrid dream would come to an end! Mary could hear her breath, loud and uneven from crying, inside the dream. She looked at her reflection. For a moment the breathing, and everything with it, stopped. She saw herself in the glass with a hideous roundness above that belonged to a nightmare, not to a human being. Her chest was round and horrible and enormous, and, as if it wanted to escape from that prison, her heart struggled wildly inside it, beating until it hurt. She couldn't bear to look in the glass, she had no more eyes: and suddenly she seemed to be in another dark place where something was struggling because it was frightened, and a panting, fluttering breath gasped to save it.

The two unimportant ladies who came to tea possessed no car of their own. 'So kind'; 'Most thoughtful,' they twittered together, when her ladyship offered the Buick to drive them home. The long, sleek shining car, the symbol of wealth and power, fascinated them, rolling smoothly to the front door, the fat white-painted tyres softly crunching the gravel. For a moment they stood with their hostess between the potted hydrangeas outside the door, admiring the car and the good-looking chauffeur, smart as a naval man in dark blue and a white-topped cap.

Suddenly there was a distraction, something made them look up. At one of the upper windows of the great house a kind of indistinct flurry was going on, as if a distraught trapped bird were struggling there. Peering, they distinguished a small form crouched on the window-sill, a white face pressed against the mosquito wire.

'James! The baby pigeon – it's been thrown out again. Save it! James!'

From up there came these queer plaintive desperate cries.

The driver, involved with his purring engine, seemed unaware. The visitors glanced from him to the woman between the hydrangeas, whose stiffened face told them they had witnessed something not meant for their eyes and ears. Diplomatically, they hurried into their seats, pretending they had noticed nothing, calling out thin goodbyes.

The car moved forward at once, the two heads inside swung round simultaneously. Mammoth arms closed round the figure at the window and lifted it bodily out of their sight. Down came the blind. The eyes of the window went dead.

Gathering speed, the Buick carried the ladies quickly towards the gates. Each gave the other a lengthy and knowing look.

'So that's it! Her keeper – I often wondered about that great hulking maid; like a wardress,' murmured one of them to her friend, cautiously eyeing the chauffeur's straight back, hoping he could not hear.

Illustration by Marguerite McBey,
from the novella *Too Far From Home*
by Paul Bowles

Paul Bowles

PAUL BOWLES was born in New England in 1910. He came to Europe from New York in 1931 to study music – his first vocation – with Aaron Copland and, in 1938, married Jane Auer, herself a gifted writer who achieved international fame under her married name of Jane Bowles. After the war they settled in Tangier, which remained Paul Bowles's permanent home until his death in 1999. Renowned for his unforgettable first novel *The Sheltering Sky*, he wrote three other widely acclaimed novels – *Let It Come Down*, *The Spider's House* and *Up Above the World* – as well as short stories and travel pieces, all of which confirm his reputation as a writer of exceptional talent and distinction who deserves his reputation as one of the most powerful writers in English in the twentieth century.

'Bowles was a man who brought together the Lost Generation of the Twenties, the radical art of the Thirties, the New York vanguard of the Forties, the Beat Generation of the Fifties and the Underground of the Sixties.' – *The Times*

The Delicate Prey

This story is taken from the collection *Pages From Cold Point*, first published by Peter Owen in 1968.

THERE WERE THREE Filala who sold leather in Tabelbala – two brothers and the young son of their sister. The two older merchants were serious, bearded men who liked to engage in complicated theological discussions during the slow passage of the hot hours in their *hanoute* near the market-place; the youth naturally occupied himself almost exclusively with the black-skinned girls in the small *quartier réservé*. There was one who seemed more desirable than the others, so that he was a little sorry when the older men announced that soon they would all leave for Tessalit. But nearly every town has its *quartier*, and Driss was reasonably certain of being able to have any lovely resident of any *quartier*, whatever her present emotional entanglements; thus his chagrin at hearing of the projected departure was short-lived.

The three Filala waited for the cold weather before starting out for Tessalit. Because they wanted to get there quickly they chose the westernmost trail, which is also the one leading through the most remote regions, contiguous to the lands of the plundering Reguibat tribes. It had been a long time since the uncouth men from the uplands had swept down from the *hammada* upon a caravan; most people were of the opinion that since the war of the Sarrho they had lost the greater part of their arms and ammunition, and, more important still, their spirit. And a tiny group of three men and their camels could scarcely awaken the envy of the Reguibat, traditionally rich with loot from all Rio de Oro and Mauritania.

Their friends in Tabelbala, most of them other Filali leather merchants, walked beside them sadly as far as the edge of the town; then they bade them farewell, and watched them mount their camels to ride off slowly toward the bright horizon.

'If you meet any Reguibat, keep them ahead of you!' they called.

The danger lay principally in the territory they would reach only three or four days' journey from Tabelbala; after a week the edge of the land haunted by the Reguibat would be left entirely behind. The weather was cool save at midday. They took turns sitting guard at night; when Driss stayed awake he brought out a small flute whose piercing notes made the older uncle frown with annoyance, so that he asked him to go and sit at some distance from the sleeping-blankets. All night he sat playing whatever sad songs he could call to mind; the bright ones in his opinion belonged to the *quartier*, where one was never alone.

When the uncles kept watch, they sat quietly, staring ahead of them into the night. There were just the three of them.

And then one day a solitary figure appeared, moving toward them across the lifeless plains from the west. One man on a camel; there was no sign of any others, although they scanned the wasteland in every direction. They stopped for a while; he altered his course slightly. They went ahead; he changed it again. There was no doubt that he wanted to speak with them.

'Let him come,' grumbled the older uncle, glaring about the empty horizon once more. 'We each have a gun.'

Driss laughed. To him it seemed absurd even to admit the possibility of trouble from one lone man.

When finally the figure arrived within calling distance, it hailed them in a voice like a muezzin's: '*S'l'm aleikoum!*' They halted, but did not dismount, and waited for the man to draw nearer. Soon he called again. This time the uncle replied, but the distance was still too great for his voice to carry, and the man did not hear his greeting. Presently he was close enough for them to see that he did not wear Reguiba attire. They muttered to one another: 'He comes from the north, not the west.' And they all felt glad. However, even when he came up beside them they remained on the camels, bowing solemnly from where they sat and always searching in the new face, and in the garments below it, for some false note which might reveal the possible truth – that the man was a scout for the Reguibat, who would be waiting up on the *hammada* only a few hours distant, or were even now moving parallel to the trail, closing in upon them in such a manner that they would not arrive at a point within visibility until after dusk.

Certainly the stranger himself was no Reguiba. He was quick and jolly, with light skin and very little beard. It occurred to Driss that he did not like his small, active eyes which seemed to take in everything and give out nothing, but this passing reaction became only a part of the general initial distrust, all of which was dissipated when they learned that the man was a Moungari. Moungar is a holy place in that part of the world, and its few residents are treated with respect by the pilgrims who go to visit the ruined shrine nearby.

The newcomer took no pains to hide the fear he had felt at being alone in the region, or the pleasure it gave him to be now with three other men. They all dismounted and made tea to seal their friendship, the Moungari furnishing the charcoal.

During the third round of glasses he made the suggestion that, since he was going more or less in their direction, he accompany them as far as Taoudeni. His bright black eyes darting from one Filali to the other, he explained that he was an excellent shot; he was certain he could supply them all with some good gazelle meat en route, or at least an *aoudad*. The Filala considered; the oldest finally said. 'Agreed.' Even if the Moungari turned out to have not quite the hunting prowess he claimed for himself, there would be four of them on the voyage instead of three.

Two mornings later, in the mighty silence of the rising sun, the Moungari pointed at the low hills that lay beside them to the east. '*Timma*. I know this land. Wait here. If you hear me shoot, then come, because that will mean there are gazelles.'

The Moungari went off on foot, climbing up between the boulders and disappearing behind the nearest crest. 'He trusts us,' thought the Filala. 'He has left his *mehari*, his blankets, his packs.' They said nothing, but each knew that the others were thinking the same as he, and they all felt warmly toward this stranger. They sat waiting in the early morning chill while the camels grumbled.

It seemed unlikely that there would prove to be any gazelles in the region, but if there should be any, and the Moungari were as good a hunter as he claimed to be, then there was a chance they would have a *mechoui* of gazelle that evening, and that would be very fine.

Slowly the sun mounted in the hard blue sky. One camel lumbered up and went off, hoping to find a dead thistle or a bush between the rocks, something left over from a year when rain may have fallen. When it had disappeared, Driss went in search of it and drove it back to the others, shouting '*Hut!*'

He sat down. Suddenly there came a shot, a long empty interval, and then another shot. The sounds were fairly distant, but perfectly clear in the absolute silence. The older brother said: 'I shall go. Who knows? There may be many gazelles.' He clambered up the rocks, the gun in his hand, and was gone.

Again they waited. When the shots sounded this time, they came from two guns.

'Perhaps they have killed one!' Driss cried.

'*Yemkin*. With Allah's aid,' replied his uncle, rising and taking up his gun. 'I want to try my hand at this.'

Driss was disappointed: he had hoped to go himself. If only he had got up a moment ago it might have been possible, but even so it was likely that he would have been left behind to watch the *mehara*. In any case, now it was too late; his uncle had spoken.

'Good.'

His uncle went off singing a song from Tafilalet, about date-palms and hidden smiles. For several minutes Driss heard snatches of the song as the melody reached the high notes. Then the sound was lost in the enveloping silence.

He waited. The sun was becoming very hot. He covered his head with his burnoose. The camels looked at each other stupidly, craning their necks, baring their brown and yellow teeth. He thought of playing his flute, but it did not seem the right moment: he was too restless, too eager to be up there with his gun, crouching behind the rocks, stalking the delicate prey. He thought of Tessalit and wondered what it would be like. Full of Blacks and Touareg, certainly more lively than Tabelbala because of the road that passed through it. There was a shot. He waited for others, but no more came this time. Again he imagined himself there among the boulders, taking aim at a fleeing beast. He pulled the trigger, the animal fell. Others appeared, and he got them all. In the dark the travellers sat around the fire gorging themselves with the rich roasted flesh, their faces gleaming with grease. Everyone was happy, and even the Moungari admitted that the young Filali was the best hunter of them all.

In the advancing heat he dozed, his mind playing over a landscape made of soft thighs and small hard breasts rising like sand dunes; wisps of song floated like clouds in the sky, and the air was thick with the taste of fat gazelle meat.

He sat up and looked around quickly. The camels lay with their necks stretched along the ground in front of them. Nothing had changed. He stood up, uneasily scanning the stony landscape. While he had slept, a hostile presence had entered into his consciousness. Translating into thought what he already sensed, he cried out. Since first he had seen those small, active eyes he had felt mistrustful of their owner, but the fact that his uncles had accepted him had pushed suspicion away into the dark of his mind. Now, unleashed in slumber, it had bounded back. He turned toward the hot hillside and looked intently between the boulders into the black shadows. In memory he heard again the shots up among the rocks, and he knew what they had meant. Catching his breath in a sob, he ran to mount his *mehari*, forced it up, and already had gone several hundred paces before he was aware of what he was doing. He stopped the animal and sat

53

quietly a moment, glancing back at the campsite with fear and indecision. If his uncles were dead, then there was nothing to do but get out into the open desert as quickly as possible, away from the rocks that could hide the Moungari while he took aim.

And so, not knowing the way to Tessalit, and without sufficient food or water, he started ahead, lifting one hand from time to time to wipe away the tears.

For two or three hours he continued that way, scarcely noticing where the *mehari* walked. All at once he sat erect, uttered an oath against himself, and in a fury turned the beast around. At that very moment his uncles might be seated in the camp with the Moungari, preparing a *mechoui* and a fire, sadly asking themselves why their nephew had deserted them. Or perhaps one would already have set out in search of him. There would be no possible excuse for his conduct, which had been the result of an absurd terror. As he thought about it, his anger against himself mounted: he had behaved in an unforgivable manner. Noon had passed; the sun was in the west. It would be late when he got back. At the prospect of the inevitable reproaches and the mocking laughter that would greet him, he felt his face grow hot with shame, and he kicked the *mehari*'s flanks viciously.

A good while before he arrived at the camp he heard singing. This surprised him. He halted and listened: the voice was too far away to be identified, but Driss felt certain it was the Moungari's. He continued around the side of the hill to a spot in full view of the camels. The singing stopped, leaving silence. Some of the packs had been loaded back on to the beasts, preparatory to setting out. The sun had sunk low, and the shadows of the rocks were stretched out along the earth. There was no sign that they had caught any game. He called out, ready to dismount. Almost at the same instant there was a shot from very nearby, and he heard the small rushing sound of a bullet go past his head. He seized his gun. There was another shot, a sharp pain in his arm, and his gun slipped to the ground.

For a moment he sat there holding his arm, dazed. Then

swiftly he leaped down and remained crouching among the stones, reaching out with his good arm for the gun. As he touched it, there was a third shot, and the rifle moved along the ground a few inches toward him in a small cloud of dust. He drew back his hand and looked at it: it was dark and blood dripped from it. At that moment the Moungari bounded across the open space between them. Before Driss could rise the man was upon him, had pushed him back down to the ground with the barrel of his rifle. The untroubled sky lay above; the Moungari glanced up at it defiantly. He straddled the supine youth, thrusting the gun into his neck just below the chin, and under his breath he said: 'Filali dog!'

Driss stared up at him with a certain curiosity. The Moungari had the upper hand; Driss could only wait. He looked at the face in the sun's light, and discovered a peculiar intensity there. He knew the expression: it comes from hashish. Carried along on its hot fumes, a man can escape very far from the world of meaning. To avoid the malevolent face he rolled his eyes from side to side. There was only the fading sky. The gun was choking him a little. He whispered: 'Where are my uncles?'

The Moungari pushed harder against his throat with the gun, leaned partially over and with one hand ripped away his *serouelle*, so that he lay naked from the waist down, squirming a little as he felt the cold stones beneath him.

Then the Moungari drew forth rope and bound his feet. Taking two steps to his head, he abruptly faced in the other direction, and thrust the gun into his navel. Still with one hand, he slipped the remaining garments off over the youth's head and lashed his wrists together. With an old barber's razor he cut off the superfluous rope. During this time Driss called his uncles by name, loudly, first one and then the other.

The man moved and surveyed the young body lying on the stones. He ran his finger along the razor's blade; a pleasant excitement took possession of him. He stepped over, looked down, and saw the sex that sprouted from the base of the belly.

Not entirely conscious of what he was doing, he took it in one hand and brought his other arm down with the motion of a reaper wielding a sickle. It was swiftly severed. A round, dark hole was left, flush with the skin; he stared a moment, blankly. Driss was screaming. The muscles all over his body stood out, moved.

Slowly the Moungari smiled, showing his teeth. He put his hand on the hard belly and smoothed the skin. Then he made a small vertical incision there, and using both hands, studiously stuffed the loose organ in until it disappeared.

As he was cleaning his hands in the sand, one of the camels uttered a sudden growling gurgle. The Moungari leaped up and wheeled about savagely, holding his razor high in the air. Then, ashamed of his nervousness, feeling that Driss was watching and mocking him (although the youth's eyes were unseeing with pain), he kicked him over on to his stomach where he lay making small spasmodic movements. And as the Moungari followed these with his eyes, a new idea came to him. It would be pleasant to inflict an ultimate indignity upon the young Filali. He threw himself down; this time he was vociferous and leisurely in his enjoyment. Eventually he slept.

At dawn he awoke and reached for his razor, lying on the ground nearby. Driss moaned faintly. The Moungari turned him over and pushed the blade back and forth with a sawing motion into his neck, until he was certain he had severed the windpipe. Then he rose, walked away, and finished the loading of the camels he had started the day before. When this was done he spent a good while dragging the body over to the base of the hill and concealing it there among the rocks.

In order to transport the Filala's merchandise to Tessalit (for in Taoudeni there would be no buyers), it was necessary to take their *mehara* with him. It was nearly fifty days later when he arrived. Tessalit is a small town. When the Moungari began to show the leather around, an old Filali living there, whom the people called Ech Chibani, got wind of his presence. As a prospective buyer he came to examine the hides, and the Moungari was unwise enough to let him see them. Filali leather is unmistakable, and only the Filala buy and sell it in quantity. Ech Chibani knew the Moungari had come by it illicitly, but he said nothing. When a few days later another caravan arrived from Tabelbala with friends of the three Filala who asked after them, and showed great distress on hearing that they never had arrived, the old man went to the Tribunal. After some difficulty, he found a Frenchman who was willing to listen to him. The next day the Commandant and two subordinates paid the Moungari a visit. They asked him how he happened to have the three extra *mehara*, which still carried some of their Filali trappings; his replies took a devious turn. The Frenchmen listened seriously, thanked him, and left. He did not see the Commandant wink at the others as they went out into the street. And so he remained sitting in his courtyard, not knowing that he had been judged and found guilty.

The three Frenchmen went back to the Tribunal where the newly arrived Filali merchants were sitting with Ech Chibani. The story had an old pattern; there was no doubt at all about the Moungari's guilt. 'He is yours,' said the Commandant. 'Do what you like with him.'

The Filala thanked him profusely, held a short conference with the aged Chibani, and strode out in a group. When they arrived at the Moungari's dwelling he was making tea. He looked up, and a chill moved along his spine. He began to scream his innocence at them; they said nothing, but at the point of a rifle bound him and tossed him into a corner, where he continued to babble and sob. Quietly, they drank the tea he had been brewing, made some more, and went out at twilight. They tied him to one of the *mehara*, and mounting their own, moved in a silent procession (silent save for the Moungari) out through the town gate into the infinite wasteland beyond.

Half the night they continued, until they were in a completely unfrequented region of the desert. While he lay raving, bound to the camel, they dug a well-like pit, and when they had finished they lifted him off, still trussed tightly, and stood him in it. Then they filled all the space around his body with sand and stones, until only his head remained above the earth's surface. In the faint light of the new moon his shaved pate without its turban looked rather like a rock. And still he pleaded with them, calling upon Allah and Sidi Ahmed ben Moussa to witness his innocence. But he might have been singing a song for all the attention they paid to his words. Presently they set off for Tessalit; in no time they were out of hearing.

When they had gone the Moungari fell silent, to wait through the cold hours for the sun that would bring first warmth, then heat, thirst, fire, visions. The next night he did not know where he was, did not feel the cold. The wind blew dust along the ground into his mouth as he sang.

Illustration by Michael McCurdy, from *The Man Who Planted Trees* by Jean Giono

Jane Bowles

JANE BOWLES, née Auer, was born in New York in 1917. Always unconventional, she alarmed her mother by frequenting inter-racial lesbian bars at a young age. She was married to Paul Bowles in 1937, with whom she lived in many parts of the world, most famously in Tangier. They had an open relationship, each allowing the other to pursue outside liaisons and often not living together, yet always maintaining a bond. Her novel *Two Serious Ladies* was first published in the USA in 1943; subsequently reissued by Peter Owen in 1965, it became an international success. She was also the author of a volume of stories entitled *Plain Pleasures* and a play, *In the Summer House*. Plagued by ill health for much of her life, she suffered a stroke in 1957 which left her almost unable to write, thus exacerbating her already chronic writer's block. Some attributed her decline in health to her having been poisoned by her Moroccan lover, Cherifa. This relationship mystified many of Bowles's friends, who found Cherifa surly and avaricious, with some unaccountable hold over Bowles. Jane Bowles died in a psychiatric institution in Málaga in 1973, where she had been an inmate since the late 1960s.

'Jane Bowles is a remarkable figure, not only because of the brilliance of her surreal prose but for the ways in which she fought the world, and lost.' – *Observer*

Everything Is Nice

This story is taken from the collection *Plain Pleasures*, first published by Peter Owen in 1966.

THE HIGHEST STREET in the blue Moslem town skirted the edge of a cliff. She walked over to the thick protecting wall and looked down. The tide was out, and the flat dirty rocks below were swarming with skinny boys. A Moslem woman came up to the blue wall and stood next to her, grazing her hip with the basket she was carrying. She pretended not to notice her, and kept her eyes fixed on a white dog that had just slipped down the side of a rock and plunged into a crater of sea water. The sound of its bark was earsplitting. Then the woman jabbed the basket firmly into her ribs, and she looked up.

'That one is a porcupine,' said the woman, pointing a henna-stained finger into the basket.

This was true. A large dead porcupine lay there, with a pair of new yellow socks folded on top of it.

She looked again at the woman. She was dressed in a haik, and the white cloth covering the lower half of her face was loose, about to fall down.

'I am Zodelia,' she announced in a high voice. 'And you are Betsoul's friend.' The loose cloth slipped below her chin and hung there like a bib. She did not pull it up.

'You sit in her house and you sleep in her house and you eat in her house,' the woman went on, and she nodded in agreement. 'Your name is Jeanie and you live in a hotel with other Nazarenes. How much does the hotel cost you?'

A loaf of bread shaped like a disc flopped on to the ground from inside the folds of the woman's haik, and she did not have to

61

answer her question. With some difficulty the woman picked the loaf up and stuffed it in between the quills of the porcupine and the basket handle. Then she set the basket down on the top of the blue wall and turned to her with bright eyes.

'I am the people in the hotel,' she said. 'Watch me.'

She was pleased because she knew that the woman who called herself Zodelia was about to present her with a little skit. It would be delightful to watch, since all the people of the town spoke and gesticulated as though they had studied at the *Comédie Française*.

'The people in the hotel,' Zodelia announced, formally beginning her skit. 'I am the people in the hotel.

'"Goodbye, Jeanie, goodbye. Where are you going?"

'"I am going to a Moslem house to visit my Moslem friends, Betsoul and her family. I will sit in a Moslem room and eat Moslem food and sleep on a Moslem bed."

'"Jeanie, Jeanie, when will you come back to us in the hotel and sleep in your own room?"

'"I will come back to you in three days. I will come back and sit in a Nazarene room and eat Nazarene food and sleep on a Nazarene bed. I will spend half the week with Moslem friends and half with Nazarenes."'

The woman's voice had a triumphant ring as she finished her sentence; then, without announcing the end of the sketch, she walked over to the wall and put one arm around her basket.

Down below, just at the edge of the cliff's shadow, a Moslem woman was seated on a rock, washing her legs in one of the holes filled with sea water. Her haik was piled on her lap and she was huddled over it, examining her feet.

'She is looking at the ocean,' said Zodelia.

She was not looking at the ocean; with her head down and the mass of cloth in her lap she could not possibly have seen it; she would have had to straighten up and turn around.

'She is *not* looking at the ocean,' she said.

'She is looking at the ocean,' Zodelia repeated, as if she had not spoken.

She decided to change the subject. 'Why do you have a porcupine with you?' she asked her, although she knew that some of the Moslems, particularly the country people, enjoyed eating them.

'It is a present for my aunt. Do you like it?'

'Yes,' she said. 'I like porcupines. I like big porcupines and little ones, too.'

Zodelia seemed bewildered, and then bored, and she decided she had somehow ruined the conversation by mentioning small porcupines.

'Where is your mother?' Zodelia said at length.

'My mother is in her country in her own house,' she said automatically; she had answered the question a hundred times.

'Why don't you write her a letter and tell her to come here? You can take her on a promenade and show her the ocean. After that she can go back to her own country and sit in her house.' She picked up her basket and adjusted the strip of cloth over her mouth. 'Would you like to go to a wedding?' she asked her.

She said she would love to go to a wedding, and they started off down the crooked blue street, heading into the wind. As they passed a small shop Zodelia stopped. 'Stand here,' she said. 'I want to buy something.'

After studying the display for a minute or two Zodelia poked her and pointed to some cakes inside a square box with glass sides. 'Nice?' she asked her. 'Or not nice?'

The cakes were dusty and coated with a thin, ugly-coloured icing. They were called *Galletas Ortiz*.

'They are very nice,' she replied, and bought her a dozen of them. Zodelia thanked her briefly and they walked on. Presently they turned off the street into a narrow alley and started downhill. Soon Zodelia stopped at a door on the right, and lifted the heavy brass knocker in the form of a fist.

'The wedding is here?' she said to her.

Zodelia shook her head and looked grave. 'There is no wedding here,' she said.

A child opened the door and quickly hid behind it, covering

her face. She followed Zodelia across the black and white tile floor of the closed patio. The walls were washed in blue, and a cold light shone through the broken panes of glass far above their heads. There was a door on each side of the patio. Out side one of them, barring the threshold, was a row of pointed slippers. Zodelia stepped out of her own shoes and set them down near the others.

She stood behind Zodelia and began to take off her own shoes. It took her a long time because there was a knot in one of her laces. When she was ready, Zodelia took her hand and pulled her along with her into a dimly lit room, where she led her over to a mattress which lay against the wall.

'Sit,' she told her, and she obeyed. Then, without further comment she walked off, heading for the far end of the room. Because her eyes had not grown used to the dimness, she had the impression of a figure disappearing down a long corridor. Then she began to see the brass bars of a bed, glowing weakly in the darkness.

Only a few feet away, in the middle of the carpet, sat an old lady in a dress made of green and purple curtain fabric. Through the many rents in the material she could see the printed cotton dress and the tan sweater underneath. Across the room several women sat along another mattress, and further along the mattress three babies were sleeping in a row, each one close against the wall with its head resting on a fancy cushion.

'Is it nice here?' It was Zodelia, who had returned without her haik. Her black crêpe European dress hung unbelted down to her ankles, almost grazing her bare feet. The hem was lopsided. 'Is it nice here?' she asked again, crouching on her haunches in front of her and pointing at the old woman. 'That one is Tetum,' she said. The old lady plunged both hands into a bowl of raw chopped meat and began shaping the stuff into little balls.

'Tetum,' echoed the ladies on the mattress.

'This Nazarene,' said Zodelia, gesturing in her direction, 'spends half her time in a Moslem house with Moslem friends and the other half in a Nazarene hotel with other Nazarenes.'

'That's nice,' said the women opposite. 'Half with Moslem friends and half with Nazarenes.'

The old lady looked very stern, She noticed that her bony cheeks were tattooed with tiny blue crosses.

'Why?' asked the old lady abruptly in a deep voice. '*Why* does she spend half her time with Moslem friends and half with Nazarenes?' She fixed her eye on Zodelia, never ceasing to shape the meat with her swift fingers. Now she saw that her knuckles were also tattooed with blue crosses.

Zodelia stared back at her stupidly. 'I don't know why,' she said, shrugging one fat shoulder. It was clear that the picture she had been painting for them had suddenly lost all its charm for her.

'Is she crazy?' the old lady asked.

'No,' Zodelia answered listlessly. 'She is not crazy.' There were shrieks of laughter from the mattress.

The old lady fastened her sharp eyes on the visitor, and she saw that they were heavily outlined in black. 'Where is your husband?' she demanded.

'He's travelling in the desert.'

'Selling things,' Zodelia put in. This was the popular explanation for her husband's trips; she did not try to contradict it.

'Where is your mother?' the old lady asked.

'My mother is in our country in her own house.'

'Why don't you go and sit with your mother in her own house?' she scolded. 'The hotel costs a lot of money.'

'In the city where I was born,' she began, 'there are many, many automobiles and many, many trucks.'

The women on the mattress were smiling pleasantly. 'Is that true?' remarked the one in the centre in a tone of polite interest.

'I hate trucks,' she told the woman with feeling.

The old lady lifted the bowl of meat off her lap and set it down on the carpet. 'Trucks are nice,' she said severely.

'That's true,' the women agreed, after only a moment's hesitation. 'Trucks are very nice.'

'Do *you* like trucks?' she asked Zodelia, thinking that because of their relatively greater intimacy she might perhaps agree with her.

'Yes,' she said. 'They are nice. Trucks are very nice.' She seemed lost in meditation, but only for an instant. 'Everything is nice,' she announced, with a look of triumph.

'It's the truth,' the women said from their mattress. 'Every thing is nice.'

They all looked happy, but the old lady was still frowning. 'Aicha!' she yelled, twisting her neck so that her voice could be heard in the patio. 'Bring the tea!'

Several little girls came into the room carrying the tea things and a low round table.

'Pass the cakes to the Nazarene,' she told the smallest child, who was carrying a cut-glass dish piled with cakes. She saw that they were the ones she had bought for Zodelia; she did not want any of them. She wanted to go home.

'Eat!' the women called out from their mattress. 'Eat the cakes.'

The child pushed the glass dish forward.

'The dinner at the hotel is ready,' she said, standing up.

'Drink tea,' said the old woman scornfully. 'Later you will sit with the other Nazarenes and eat their food.'

'The Nazarenes will be angry if I'm late.' She realized that she was lying stupidly, but she could not stop. 'They will hit me!' She tried to look wild and frightened.

'Drink tea. They will not hit you,' the old woman told her. 'Sit down and drink tea.'

The child was still offering her the glass dish as she backed away toward the door. Outside she sat down on the black and white tiles to lace her shoes. Only Zodelia followed her into the patio.

'Come back,' the others were calling. 'Come back into the room.'

Then she noticed the porcupine basket standing nearby against the wall. 'Is that old lady in the room your aunt? Is she the one you were bringing the porcupine to?' she asked her.

'No. She is not my aunt.'

'Where *is* your aunt?'

'My aunt is in her own house.'

'When will you take the porcupine to her?' She wanted to keep talking, so that Zodelia would be distracted and forget to fuss about her departure.

'The porcupine sits here,' she said firmly. 'In my own house.'

She decided not to ask her again about the wedding.

When they reached the door Zodelia opened it just enough to let her through. 'Goodbye,' she said behind her. 'I shall see you tomorrow, if Allah wills it.'

'When?'

'Four o'clock.' It was obvious that she had chosen the first figure that had come into her head. Before closing the door she reached out and pressed two of the dry Spanish cakes into her hand. 'Eat them,' she said graciously. 'Eat them at the hotel with the other Nazarenes.'

She started up the steep alley, headed once again for the walk along the cliff. The houses on either side of her were so close that she could smell the dampness of the walls and feel it on her cheeks like a thicker air.

When she reached the place where she had met Zodelia she went over to the wall and leaned on it. Although the sun had sunk behind the houses, the sky was still luminous and the blue of the wall had deepened. She rubbed her fingers along it: the wash was fresh and a little of the powdery stuff came off. And she remembered how once she had reached out to touch the face of a clown because it had awakened some longing. It had happened at a little circus, but not when she was a child.

Grandmother by Marc Chagall, from his autobiography *My Life*

Tarjei Vesaas

TARJEI VESAAS was born on a farm in the small village of Vinje in Telemark, an isolated mountainous district of southern Norway, in 1897 and, having little taste for travel and an abiding love of his native country-side, died there in 1976 aged seventy-two. A modernist who wrote, against literary convention, in Nynorsk rather than the Danish-influenced literary language Bokmål, he is regarded as one of Norway's greatest twentieth-century writers. The author of more than twenty-five novels, five books of poetry, plus plays and short stories, he was three times a Nobel Prize candidate, though he never won the laureate. He did, however, receive Scandinavia's most important literary award, the Nordic Council Literature Prize. He first began writing in the 1920s, but he did not gain international recognition until the mid-1960s, when Peter Owen first published his books in translation; since then they have appeared in many languages. Doris Lessing described *The Ice Palace* as a 'truly beautiful book . . . poetic, delicate, unique, unforgettable, extraordinary'. The other work of fiction which, together with this novel, is generally regarded as his best is *The Birds*. At the time of his death he was considered Scandinavia's leading writer, and to this day coachloads of his fans go on pilgrimages to his old farmhouse home.

'A novelist of true visionary power.' – *Sunday Telegraph*

The Ice Palace

This is an extract from *The Ice Palace*, the story of two eleven-year-old girls, Unn and Siss. Unn is about to reveal a secret, one that leads to her death in the palace of ice surrounding a frozen waterfall. Siss's struggle with her fidelity to the memory of her friend, the strange, terrifyingly beautiful frozen chambers of the waterfall and Unn's fatal exploration of the ice palace are described in prose of lyrical economy that ranks among the most memorable achievements of modern literature. In 1973 Vesaas was awarded the Nordic Council Prize for the novel.

THE ROAR WAS suddenly stronger. The river began to quicken its speed, flowing in yellow channels. Unn ran down the slope alongside, in a silvered confusion of heather and grass tussocks, an occasional tree among them. The roar was stronger, thick whorls of spray rose up abruptly in front of her – she was at the top of the falls.

She stopped short as if about to fall over the edge, so abruptly did it appear.

Two waves went through her: first the paralysing cold, then the reviving warmth – as happens on great occasions.

Unn was there for the first time. No one had asked her to come here with them during the summer. Auntie had mentioned that there was a waterfall, no more. There had been no discussion of it until now, in the late autumn at school, after the ice palace had come and was worth seeing.

And what was this?

It must be the ice palace.

The sun had suddenly disappeared. There was a ravine with steep sides; the sun would perhaps reach into it later, but now it was in ice-cold shadow. Unn looked down into an enchanted world of small pinnacles, gables, frosted domes, soft curves and confused tracery. All of it was ice, and the water spurted between, building it up continually. Branches of the waterfall had been diverted and rushed into new channels, creating new forms. Everything shone. The sun had not yet come, but it shone ice-blue and green of itself, and deathly cold. The waterfall plunged into the middle of it as if diving into a black cellar. Up on the edge of the rock the water spread out in stripes, the colour changing from black to green, from green to yellow and white, as the fall became wilder. A booming came from the cellar-hole where the water dashed itself into white foam against the stones on the bottom. Huge puffs of mist rose into the air.

Unn began to shout for joy. It was drowned in the surge and din, just as her warm clouds of breath were swallowed up by the cold spume.

The spume and the spray at each side did not stop for an instant, but went on building minutely and surely, although frenziedly. The water was taken out of its course to build with the help of the frost: larger, taller, alcoves and passages and alleyways, and domes of ice above them; far more intricate and splendid than anything Unn had ever seen before.

She was looking right down on it. She had to see it from below, and she began to climb down the steep, rimed slope at the side of the waterfall. She was completely absorbed by the palace, so stupendous did it appear to her.

Only when she was down at the foot of it did she see it as a little girl on the ground would see it, and every scrap of guilty conscience vanished. She could not help thinking that nothing had been more right than to go there. The enormous ice palace proved to be seven times bigger and more extravagant from this angle.

From here the ice walls seemed to touch the sky; they grew as she thought about them. She was intoxicated. The palace was full of wings and turrets, how many it was impossible to say. The water had made it swell in all directions, and the main waterfall plunged down in the middle, keeping a space clear for itself.

There were places that the water had abandoned, so that they were completed, shining and dry. Others were covered in spume

71

and water drops, and trickling moisture that in a flash turned into blue-green ice.

It was an enchanted palace. She must try to find a way in! It was bound to be full of curious passages and doorways – and she must get in. It looked so extraordinary that Unn forgot everything else as she stood in front of it. She was aware of nothing but her desire to enter.

But finding the way was not so simple. Many places that looked like openings cheated her, but she did not give up, and so she found a fissure with water trickling through it, wide enough to squeeze herself through.

Unn's heart was thudding as she entered the first room.

Green, with shafts of subdued light penetrating here and there; empty but for the biting cold. There was something sinister about the room.

Without thinking she shouted 'Hey!', calling for someone. The emptiness had that effect; you had to shout in it. She did not know why, she knew there was nobody there.

The reply came at once. 'Hey!' answered the room weakly. How she started!

One might have expected the room to be as quiet as the tomb, but it was filled with an even roaring. The noise of the waterfall penetrated the mass of ice. The wild play of the water outside, dashing itself to foam against the stones on the bottom, was a low, dangerous churning in here.

Unn stood for a little to let her fright ebb away. She did not know what she had called to and did not know what had answered her. It could not have been an ordinary echo.

Perhaps the room was not so large after all? It felt large. She did not try to see whether she could get more answers; instead she looked for a way out, a means of getting further in. It did not occur to her for a moment to squeeze out into the daylight again.

And she found a way as soon as she looked for it: a large fissure between polished columns of ice.

She emerged into a room that was more like a passage, but was a room all the same. She tested it with a half-whispered 'Hey!' and got a half-frightened 'Hey!' back again. She knew that rooms like this belonged in palaces – she was bewitched and ensnared, and let what had been lie behind her. At this moment she thought only of palaces.

She did not shout 'Siss!' in the dark passage, she shouted 'Hey!' She did not think about Siss in this unexpected enchantment, she thought about room upon room in a green ice palace, and that she must enter each one of them.

The cold was piercing, and she tried to see whether she could make big clouds with her breath, but the light was too dim. Here the noise of the waterfall came from below, but that couldn't be right? Nothing was right in such a palace, but you seemed to accept it.

She had to admit she was a little chilled and shivering, in spite of the warm coat Auntie had given her when the wintry weather had set in this autumn. But she would soon forget about it in the excitement of the next room, and the room was to be found, as surely as she was Unn.

As might be expected in a narrow room, there was a way out at the other end: green, dry ice, a fissure abandoned by the water.

When she arrived inside the next one she caught her breath at what she saw: she was in the middle of a petrified forest. An ice forest.

The water, which had spurted up here for a while, had fashioned stems and branches of ice, and small trees stuck up from the bottom among the large ones. There were things here too that could not be described as either the one or the other – but they belonged to such a place and one had to accept everything as it came. She stared wide-eyed into a strange fairy-tale. The water was roaring far away.

The room was light. No sunshine – it was probably still behind the hill – but the daylight sidled in, glimmering curiously through the ice walls. It was dreadfully cold.

But the cold was of no importance as long as she was there;

that was how it should be, this was the home of the cold. Unn looked round-eyed at the forest, and here too she gave a faltering and tentative shout: 'Hey!'

There was no reply.

She started in surprise. It didn't answer!

Everything was stone-hard ice. Everything was unusual. But it did not answer, and that was not right. She shuddered, and felt herself to be in danger.

The forest was hostile. The room was magnificent beyond belief, but it was hostile and it frightened her. She looked for a way out at once, before anything should happen. Forward or back meant nothing to her any longer; she had lost all sense of it.

And she found another fissure to squeeze through. They seemed to open up for her wherever she went. When she *was* through she was met by a new kind of light that she was to recognize from her past life: it was ordinary daylight.

She looked about her hastily, a little disappointed; it was the ordinary sky above her! No ceiling of ice, but a cold blue winter sky reassuringly high up. She was in a round room with smooth walls of ice. The water had been here, but had been channelled elsewhere afterwards.

Unn did not dare to shout 'Hey!' here. The ice forest had put a stop to that, but she stood and tested her clouds of breath in this ordinary light. She felt colder and colder when she remembered to think about it. The warmth from her walk had been used up long ago, the warmth inside her was now in these small clouds of breath. She let them rise up in quick succession.

She was about to go on, but stopped abruptly. Someone had called 'Hey!' From *that* direction. She spun round and found no one. But she had not imagined it.

She supposed that if the visitor did not call, then the room did so. She was not sure she liked it, but answered with a soft 'Hey!' really no more than a whisper.

But it made her feel better. She seemed to have done the right thing, so she took courage from it and looked round for a fissure so that she could go on at once. The roar of the falling water was loud and deep at this point; she was close to it without being able to see it. She must go on!

Unn was shivering with cold now, but she did not know it, she was much too excited. There was the opening! As soon as she wanted one it was there.

Through it quickly.

But this was unexpected too: she was standing in what looked like a room of tears.

As soon as she stepped in she felt a trickling drop on the back of her neck. The opening she had come through was so low that she had had to bend double.

It was a room of tears. The light in the glass walls was very weak, and the whole room seemed to trickle and weep with these falling drops in the half dark. Nothing had been built up there yet, the drops fell from the roof with a soft splash, down into each little pool of tears. It was all very sad.

They fell into her coat and her woollen cap. It didn't matter, but her heart was heavy as lead. It was weeping. What was it weeping for?

It must stop!

It did not stop. On the contrary, it seemed to increase. The water was coming in this direction in greater quantities, the trickling went faster, the tears fell copiously.

It began oozing down the walls. She felt as if her heart would break.

Unn knew well enough that it was water, but it was a room of tears just the same. It made her sadder and sadder: it was no use calling anyone or being called in a room like this. She did not even notice the roar of the water.

The drops turned to ice on her coat. In deep distress she tried to leave. She stumbled along the walls, and at once she found the way out – or the way in, for all she knew.

A way out which was narrower than any of the others through which she had squeezed, but which looked as if it led into a brightly lit hall. Unn could just see it, and she was wild with the desire to enter it; it seemed to be a matter of life and death.

Too narrow, she could not get through. But she had to get in. It's the thick coat, she thought, and tore off the coat and satchel, leaving them to lie there until she came back. She did not think much about that, in any case, only about getting in.

And now she managed it, slender and supple as she was, when she pushed hard enough.

The new room was a miracle, it seemed to her. The light shone strong and green through the walls and the ceiling, raising her spirits after their drenching in the tears.

Of course! Suddenly she understood, now she could see it clearly: it had been herself crying so hard in there. She did not know why, but it had been herself, plunged in her own tears.

It was nothing to bother about. It had just been a pause in the doorway as she stepped into this clean-swept room, luminous with green light. Not a drop on the ceiling here, and the roar of the waterfall was muffled. This room seemed to be made for shouting in, if you had something to shout about, a wild shout about companionship and comfort.

It gushed out; she called 'Siss!'

When she had done so she started. 'Siss!' came in answer from at least three directions.

She stood still until the shout mingled with the roar. Then she crossed the room. As she did so she thought about her mother, and about Siss, and about the other – she managed it for a very brief moment. The call had made an opening; now it slammed shut again.

Why am I here? it occurred to her, as she walked up and down. Not so many steps, she was walking more and more stiffly and unrecognizably. Why am I here? She attempted to find the solution to this riddle. Meanwhile she walked, strangely exalted, half unconscious.

She was close to the edge now: the ice laid its hand upon her.

She sensed the paralysing frost. Her coat had been left somewhere else, that was the reason. Now the cold could bore into her body as it liked. She felt herself getting frightened, and darted across to the wall to get out to her warm coat. Where had she come in?

The wall was a mountain of ice, compact and smooth. She darted across to another. How many walls were there? All was compact and smooth wherever she turned. She began shouting childishly, 'I must get out!' Immediately she found the opening.

But this palace was odd: she did not get back to her coat, she came out into something she did not like very much.

Yet another room. It was really tiny, and full of dripping icicles hanging down from the low ceiling, full of icicles growing up from the floor, and jagged walls with many angles, so thick that the green light was deadened. But the roar of the waterfall was not deadened, here it was suddenly very close, or underneath, or wherever it might be – it was like being right *inside* it.

The water trickled down the walls of this room, reminding her of the one in which she had cried. She did not cry now. The cold prevented that and blurred everything. Much was flashing through her mind, but as if in a mist; if she tried to grasp it, something else was there instead. It must have occurred to her that surely this was dangerous, she would shout loudly and challengingly the shout that was part of the ice palace: 'Hey! Hey!'

But it could scarcely be called a proper shout. Another thought laid itself across it, and she barely heard it herself. It did not carry at all; the only answer was the savage roar. The roar swept all other sounds away. Nor did it matter. Another thought, and another ray of cold had already chopped it off.

It occurred to her that the roar was like something to lie down in, just to lie down in and be carried away. As far as you wanted to – no, that one was chopped off.

The floor was wet with the drops. In some places the surface of the water was freezing thinly. *This* was no place to be – Unn searched the complicated walls yet again for an opening.

This was the last room; she could go no further.

She thought this only vaguely. At any rate there was no way out. This time it was no use, whatever she did. There were plenty of fissures, but they did not lead out to anything, only further in to ice and strange flashes of light.

But she had come in, after all?

No use thinking like that. It was not in, it was out now – and that was another matter, she thought confusedly. The fissure through which she had entered was naturally not to be found when she wanted to leave again.

No use calling, the roar drowned it. A hollow of tears was ready waiting in front of her. She could plunge into it, but she could not drag herself so far. She had finished with that elsewhere.

Was someone knocking on the wall?

No, nobody would knock on the wall here! You don't knock on walls of ice. What she was looking for was a dry patch to stand on.

At last she found a corner where there was no moisture, but dry frost. There she sat down with her feet tucked under her, her feet, which she could no longer feel.

Now the cold began to stiffen her whole body, and she no longer felt it so keenly. She felt tired, and had to sit down for a while before she began looking seriously for the way out and an escape – away from here – out to her coat and out to Auntie and out to Siss.

Her thoughts became gradually more confused and vague. She distinguished Mother for a while, then she slid away too. And all the rest was a mist, threaded with flashes, but not so as to hold her attention. There would be time enough to think about it later.

Everything was so long ago, it receded. She was tired of all this running about in the palace, in all this strangeness, so it was good to sit for a while, now that the cold was not troubling her so much. She sat squeezing her hands together hard. She had forgotten why. After all, she was wearing her double mitts.

The drops began to play to her. At first she had heard nothing besides the tremendous roar, but now she could distinguish the plim-plam of the falling drops. They oozed out of the low ceiling and fell on to icicles and into puddles – and there was a song in it, monotonous and incessant: plim-plam, plim-plam.

And what was *that*?

She straightened up. Something was flooding over her that she had never felt before, she began to shout – now she had a deep, black well of shouts if she should need them – but she did not let out more than one.

There was something in the ice! At first it had no form, but the moment she shouted it took shape, and shone out like an eye of ice up there, confronting her, putting a stop to her thoughts.

It was clearly an eye, a tremendous eye.

It grew wider and wider as it looked at her, right in the middle of the ice, and full of light. That was why she had shouted only once. And yet when she looked again it was not frightening.

Her thoughts were simple now. The cold had paralysed them little by little. The eye in the ice was big and looked at her unblinkingly, but there was no need to be afraid, all she thought was: What are you looking for? Here I am. More hazily a familiar thought in such situations came to her: I haven't done anything.

No need to be afraid.

She settled down again as before, with her feet drawn up, and looked about her, for the eye was bringing more light, the room was more distinct.

It's only a big eye.

There *are* big eyes here.

But she felt it looking at her from up there, and she was obliged to raise her head and meet the eye without flinching.

Here I am. I've been here all the time. I haven't done anything.

Gradually the room filled with the plim-plam of the water drops. Each drop was like a fraction of a song. Beneath played the harsh, incessant roar, and then came the high plim-plam, like more pleasant music in the middle of it. It reminded her of something she had forgotten a long time ago, and because of that it was familiar and reassuring.

The light increased.

The eye confronted her, giving out more light. But Unn looked at it boldly, letting it widen as much as it would, letting it inspect her as closely as it wished; she was not afraid of it.

She was not cold either. She was not comfortable, she was strangely paralysed, but she did not feel cold. Hazily she remembered a time when it had been dreadfully cold in the palace, but not now. She felt quite heavy and limp; she really would have liked to sleep for a little, but the eye kept her awake.

Now she no longer stirred, but sat against the wall with her head raised so that she could look straight at the light in the ice. The light became increasingly brighter and began to fill up with fire. Between herself and the eye were the quick glints of the falling drops as they made their monotonous music.

The fiery eye had been merely a warning, for now the room was suddenly drowned in flame. The winter sun was at last high enough to enter the ice palace.

The late, cold sun retained a surprising amount of its strength. Its rays penetrated thick ice walls and corners and fissures, and broke the light into wonderful patterns and colours, making the sad room dance. The icicles hanging from the ceiling and the ones growing up from the floor, and the water drops themselves all danced together in the flood of light that broke in. And the drops shone and hardened and shone and hardened, making one drop the less each time in the little room. It would soon be filled.

A blinding flood of light. Unn had lost all ties with everything but light. The staring eye had burned up, everything was light. She thought dully that there was an awful lot of it.

She was ready for sleep, she was even warm as well. It was not cold in here at any rate. The pattern in the ice wall danced in the room, the light shone more strongly. Everything that should have been upright was upside-down – everything was piercingly bright. Not once did she think this was strange; it was just as it should be. She wanted to sleep; she was languid and limp and ready.

Illustration by Ian Hugo, Anaïs Nin's husband, from Nin's collection *Under a Glass Bell*

Anaïs Nin

ANAÏS NIN was born in Paris in 1903 and moved to the USA at the age of eleven. She returned to Paris ten years later after her marriage to Hugo Guiler; there she studied analysis under Otto Rank and became acquainted with many artists and writers. Her first book was published in the 1930s, and she went on to write stories and a series of auto-biographical novels, including *Collages*, *The Four-Chambered Heart*, *A Spy in the House of Love* and *Under a Glass Bell* – from which the following story is taken – as well as her celebrated volumes of erotica, *Delta of Venus* and *Little Birds*. Perhaps best known for her journals, which were published by Peter Owen and which established her reputation, her personal life and loves have attracted considerable attention – partly through her association with Henry Miller and his wife but, not least, because for a number of years she was married to two men at the same time, one in New York and another in California, without either finding out until after her death in 1977.

'Rarely does the literature of the twentieth century reflect one of one of the great and transcending experiences: the emancipation of women. Simone de Beauvoir and Mary McCarthy have dealt with the issue . . . Anaïs Nin eclipses both of them.' – *Los Angeles Times*

Houseboat

This story is taken from the collection *Under a Glass Bell*, first published by Peter Owen in 1968.

THE CURRENT OF the crowd wanted to sweep me along with it. The green lights on the street corners ordered me to cross the street, the policeman smiled to invite me to walk between the silver-headed nails. Even the autumn leaves obeyed the current. But I broke away from it like a fallen piece. I swerved out and stood at the top of the stairs leading down to the Quays. Below me flowed the river. Not like the current I had just broken from, made of dissonant pieces colliding rustily, driven by hunger and desire.

Down the stairs I ran towards the water front, the noises of the city receding as I descended, the leaves retreating to the corner of the steps under the wind of my skirt. At the bottom of the stairs lay the wrecked mariners of the street current, the tramps who had fallen out of the crowd life, who refused to obey. Like me, at some point of the trajectory, they had all fallen out, and here they lay shipwrecked at the foot of the trees, sleeping, drinking. They had abandoned time, possessions, labour, slavery. They walked and slept in counter-rhythm to the world. They renounced houses and clothes. They sat alone, but not unique, for they all seemed to have been born brothers. Time and exposure made their clothes alike, wine and air gave them the same eroded skin. The crust of dirt, the swollen noses, the stale tears in the eyes, all gave them the same appearance. Having refused to follow the procession of the streets, they sought the river which lulled them. Wine and water. Every day, in front of the river, they re-enacted the ritual of abandon. Against the knots of rebellion, wine and the river, against the cutting iron of loneliness, wine and water washing away everything in a rhythm of blurred silences.

They threw the newspapers into the river and this was their prayer: to be carried, lifted, borne down, without feeling the hard bone of pain in man, lodged in his skeleton, but only the pulse of flowing blood. No shocks, no violence, no awakening.

While the tramps slept, the fishermen in a trance pretended to be capturing fish, and stood there hypnotized for hours. The river communicated with them through the bamboo rods of their fishing tackle, transmitting its vibrations. Hunger and time were forgotten. The perpetual waltz of lights and shadows emptied one of all memories and terrors. Fishermen, tramps, filled by the brilliance of the river as by an anaesthetic which permitted only the pulse to beat, emptied of memories as in dancing.

The houseboat was tied at the foot of the stairs. Broad and heavy on its keel, stained with patches of light and shadows, bathing in reflections, it heaved now and then to the pressure of a deeper breathing of the river. The water washed its flanks lingeringly, the moss gathered around the base of it, just below the water line, and swayed like Naiad hair, then folded back again in silky adherence to the wood. The shutters opened and closed in obedience to the gusts of wind and the heavy poles which kept the barge from touching the shore cracked with the strain like bones. A shiver passed along the houseboat asleep on the river, like a shiver of fever in a dream. The lights and shadows stopped waltzing. The nose of the houseboat plunged deeper and shook its chains. A moment of anguish: everything was slipping into anger again, as on earth. But no, the water dream persisted. Nothing was displaced. The nightmare might appear here, but the river knew the mystery of continuity. A fit of anger and only the surface erupted, leaving the deep flowing body of the dream intact.

The noises of the city receded completely as I stepped on the gangplank. As I took out the key I felt nervous. If the key fell into the river, the key to the little door to my life in the infinite? Or if the houseboat broke its moorings and floated away? It had done this once already, breaking the chain at the prow, and the tramps had helped to swing it back in place.

As soon as I was inside of the houseboat, I no longer knew the name of the river or the city. Once inside the walls of old wood, under the heavy beams, I might be inside a Norwegian sailing ship traversing fjords, in a Dutch boyer sailing to Bali, a jute boat on the Brahmaputra. At night the lights on the shore were those of Constantinople or the Neva. The giant bells ringing the hours were those of the Sunken Cathedral. Every time I inserted the key in the lock, I felt this snapping of cords, this lifting of anchor, this fever of departure. Once inside the houseboat, all the voyages began. Even at night with its shutters closed, no smoke coming out of its chimney, asleep and secret, it had an air of mysteriously sailing somewhere.

At night I closed the windows which overlooked the Quays. As I leaned over I could see dark shadows walking by, men with their collars turned up and their caps pushed over their eyes, women with wide long skirts, market women who made love with the tramps behind the trees. The street lamps high above threw no light on the trees and bushes along the big wall. It was only when the window rustled that the shadows which seemed to be one shadow split into two swiftly and then, in the silence, melted into one again.

At this moment a barge full of coal passed by, sent waves rolling behind it, upheaving all the other barges poured from his instrument, no music, but tiny plaintive cries escaped from his trembling gestures.

At the top of the stairs two policemen were chatting with the prostitutes.

The windows overlooking the Quays now shut, the barge looked uninhabited. But the windows looking on the river were open. The dying summer breath entered into my bedroom, the room of shadows, the bower of the night. Heavy beams overhead, low ceilings, a heavy wooden sideboard along the walls. An Indian lamp threw charcoal patterns over walls and ceiling – a

Persian design of cactus flowers, lace fans, palm leaves, a lamaist vajry-mandala flower, minarets, trellises.

(When I lie down to dream, it is not merely a dust flower born like a rose out of the desert sands and destroyed by a gust of wind. When I lie down to dream it is to plant the seed for the miracle and the fulfilment.)

The headboard opened like a fan over my head, a peacock feather opening in dark wood and copper threads, the wings of a great golden bird kept afloat on the river. The barge could sink, but not this wide heavy bed travelling throughout the nights spread over the deepest precipices of desire. Falling on it I felt the waves of emotion which sustained me, the constant waves of emotion under my feet. Burrowing myself into the bed only to spread fanwise and float into a moss-carpeted tunnel of caresses.

The incense was spiralling. The candles were burning. The pictures on the walls swayed. The fishing net hung on the ceiling like a giant spider web swung, gently rocking a sea shell and a starfish caught in its meshes.

On the table lay a revolver. No harm could come to me on the water but someone had laid a revolver there believing I might need it. I looked at it as if it reminded me of a crime I had committed, with an irrepressible smile such as rises sometimes to people's lips in the face of great catastrophes which are beyond their grasp, the smile which comes at times on certain women's faces while they are saying they regret the harm they have done. It is the smile of nature quietly and proudly asserting its natural right to kill, the smile which the animal in the jungle never shows but by which man reveals when the animal re-enters his being and reasserts its presence. This smile came to me as I took up the revolver and pointed it out of the window, into the river. But I was so averse to killing that even shooting into the water I felt uneasy, as if I might kill the Unknown Woman of the Seine again – the woman who had drowned her- self here years ago and who was so beautiful that at the Morgue they had taken a plaster cast of her face. The shot came faster than I had expected. The river swallowed it. No one noticed it, not from the bridge, not from the Quays. How easily a crime could be committed here.

Outside an old man was playing the violin feverishly, but no sound came out of it. He was deaf. No music with delicate oscillations of anguish. Watching them was like listening to a beloved heartbeat and fearing the golden hammer strokes might stop. The candles never conquered the darkness but maintained a disquieting duel with the night.

I heard a sound on the river, but when I leaned out of the window the river had become silent again. Now I heard the sound of oars. Softly, softly coming from the shore. A boat knocked against the barge. There was a sound of chains being tied.

I await the phantom lover – the one who haunts all women, the one I dream of, who stands behind every man, with a finger and head shaking – 'Not him, he is not the one.' Forbidding me each time to love.

The houseboat must have travelled during the night, the climate and the scenery were changed. Dawn was accelerated by a woman's shrieks. Shrieks interrupted by the sound of choking. I ran on deck. I arrived just as the woman who was drowning grasped the anchor's chain. Her shrieks grew worse as she felt nearer salvation, her appetite for life growing more violent. With the help of one of the drunken tramps, we pulled the chain up, with the woman clinging to it. She was hiccuping, spitting, choking. The drunken tramp was shouting orders to imaginary sailors, telling them what to do for the drowned. Leaning over the woman he almost toppled over her, which reawakened her aggressiveness and helped her to rise and walk into the barge where we changed her clothes.

The barge was traversing a dissonant climate. The mud had come to the surface of the river, and a shoal of corks surrounded the barge. We pushed them away with brooms and poles; the corks seemed to catch the current and float away, only to encircle the barge magnetically.

The tramps were washing themselves at the fountain. Bare to the waist, they soaked their faces and shoulders, and then they washed their shirts, and combed themselves, dipping their combs in the river. These men at the fountain, they knew what was going to happen. When they saw me on deck, they gave me the news of the day, of the approach of war, of the hope of revolution. I listened to their description of tomorrow's world. An aurora borealis and all men out of prison.

The oldest tramp of all, who did not know about tomorrow, he was in the prison of his drunkenness. No escape. When he was filled like a barrel, then his legs gave way and he could only fall down. When he was lifted by alcoholic wings and ready for flight, the wings collapsed into nausea. This gangplank of drunkenness led nowhere.

The same day at this post of anguish, three men quarrelled on the Quays. One carried a ragpicker's bag over his shoulder. The second was brilliantly elegant. The third was a beggar with a wooden leg. They argued excitedly. The elegant one was counting out money. He dropped a ten-franc piece. The beggar placed his wooden leg on it and would not budge. No one could frighten him, and no one dared to push off the wooden leg. He kept it there all the time they argued. Only when the two others went off did he lean over to pick it up.

The street cleaner was sweeping the dead leaves into the river. The rain fell into the cracked letter box and when I opened my letters it looked as if my friends had been weeping when writing me.

A child sat on the edge of the river, his thin legs dangling. He sat there for two or three hours and then began to cry. The street cleaner asked him what was the matter. His mother had told him to wait there until she returned. She had left him a piece of dry bread. He was wearing his little black school apron. The street cleaner took his comb, dipped it in the river and combed the child's hair and washed his face. I offered to take him on the barge. The street cleaner said: 'She'll never come back. That's how they do it. He's another for the Orphanage.'

When the child heard the word orphanage he ran away so fast the street cleaner did not have time to drop his broom. He shrugged his shoulders: 'They'll catch him sooner or later. I was one of them.'

Voyage of despair.

The river was having a nightmare. Its vast whaleback was restless. It had been cheated of its daily suicide. More women fed the river than men – more wanted to die in winter than in summer.

Parasitic corks obeyed every undulation but did not separate from the barge, glued like waves of mercury. When it rained the water seeped through the top room and fell on my bed, on my books, on the black rug.

I awakened in the middle of the night with wet hair. I thought I must be at the bottom of the Seine; that the barge, the bed, had quietly sunk during the night.

It was not very different to look through water at all things. It was like weeping cool saltless tears without pain. I was not cut off altogether, but in so deep a region that every element was marrying in sparkling silence, so deep that I heard the music of the spinet inside the snail who carries his antennae like an organ and travels on the back of a harp fish.

In this silence and white communion took place the convolutions of plants turning into flesh, into planets. The towers were pierced by swordfishes, the moon of citron rotated on a sky of lava, the branches had thirsty eyes hanging like berries. Tiny birds sat on weeds asking for no food and singing no song but the soft chant of metamorphosis, and each time they opened their beaks the webbed stained-glass windows decomposed into snakes and ribbons of sulphur.

The light filtered through the slabs of mildewed tombs and no eyelashes could close against it, no tears could blur it, no eyelids could curtain it off, no sleep could dissolve it, no forgetfulness could deliver one from this place where there was neither night nor day. Fish, plant, woman, equally aware, with eyes forever open, confounded and confused in communion, in an ecstasy without repose.

I ceased breathing in the present, inhaling the air around me into the leather urns of the lungs. I breathed out into the infinite, exhaling the mist of a three-quarter-tone breath, a light pyramid of heart beats.

This breathing lighter than breathing, without pressure from the wind, like the windless delicacy of the air in Chinese paintings, supporting one winged black bird, one breathless cloud, bowing one branch, preceded the white hysteria of the poet and the red-foamed hysteria of woman.

When this inhaling of particles, of dust grains, of rust microbes, of all the ashes of past deaths ceased, I inhaled the air from the unborn and felt my body like a silk scarf resting outside the blue rim of the nerves.

The body recovered the calm of minerals, its plant juices, the eyes became gems again, made to glitter alone and not for the shedding of tears.

Sleep.

No need to watch the flame of my life in the palm of my hand, this flame as pale as the holy ghost speaking in many languages to which none have the secret.

The dream will watch over it. No need to remain with eyes wide open. Now the eyes are gems, the hair a fan of lace. Sleep is upon me.

The pulp of roots, the milk of cactus, the quicksilver drippings of the silver beeches is in my veins.

I sleep with my feet on moss carpets, my branches in the cotton of the clouds.

The sleep of a hundred years has transfixed all into the silver face of ecstasy.

*

During the night the houseboat travelled out of the landscape of despair. Sunlight struck the wooden beams, and the reflected light of the water danced on the wooden beams. Opening my eyes I saw the light playing around me and I felt as if I were looking through a pierced sky into some region far nearer to the sun. Where had the houseboat sailed to during the night?

The island of joy must be near. I leaned out of the window. The moss costume of the houseboat was greener, washed by cleaner waters. The corks were gone, and the smell of rancid wine. The little waves passed with great precipitation. The waves were so clear I could see the roots of the indolent algae plants that had grown near the edge of the river.

This day I landed at the island of joy.

I could now put around my neck the sea-shell necklace and walk through the city with the arrogance of my secret.

When I returned to the houseboat with my arms loaded with new candles, wine, ink, writing paper, nails for the broken shutters, the policeman stopped me at the top of the stairs: 'Is there a holiday on the Quay?'

'A holiday? No.'

As I ran down the stairs I understood. There was a holiday on the Quay! The policeman had seen it on my face. A celebration of lights and motion. Confetti of sun spots, serpentines of water currents, music from the deaf violinist. It was the island of joy I had touched in the morning. The river and I united in a long, winding, never-ending dream, with its deep undercurrents, its deeper undertows of dark activity, the river and I rejoicing at teeming obscure mysteries of river-bottom lives.

The big clock of the Sunken Cathedral rang twelve times for the feast. Barges passed slowly in the sun, like festive chariots throwing bouquets of lightning from their highly polished knobs. The laundry in blue, white and rose, hung out to dry and waving like flags, children playing with cats and dogs, women holding the rudder with serenity and gravity. Everything washed clean with water and light passing at a dream pace.

But when I reached the bottom of the stairs the festivity came to an abrupt end. Three men were cutting the algae plants with long scythes. I shouted, but they worked on unconcerned, pushing them all away so that the current would sweep them off. The men laughed at my anger. One man said: 'These are not your plants. Cleaning Department order. Go and complain to them.'

And with quicker gestures they cut all the algae and fed the limp green carpet to the current.

So passed the barge out of the island of joy.

One morning what I found in the letter box was an order from the river police to move on. The King of England was expected for a visit and he would not like the sight of the houseboats, the laundry exposed on the decks, the chimneys and water tanks in rusty colours, the gangplanks with teeth missing, and other human flowers born of poverty and laziness. We were all ordered to sail on, quite a way up the Seine, no one knew quite where because it was all in technical language.

One of my neighbours, a one-eyed cyclist, came to discuss the dispossessions and to invoke laws which had not been made to give houseboats the right to lie in the heart of Paris gathering moss. The fat painter who lived across the river, open-shirted and always perspiring, came to discuss the matter and to suggest we do not move at all as a form of protest. What could happen? At the worst, since there were no laws against our staying, the police would have to fetch a tugboat and move us all in a line, like a row of prisoners. That was the worst that could happen to us. But the one-eyed cyclist was overcome by this threat because he said his houseboat was not strong enough to bear the strain of being pulled between other heavier, larger barges. He had heard of a small houseboat being wrenched apart in such a voyage. He did not think mine would stand the strain either.

The next day the one-eyed man was towed along by a friend who ran one of the tourist steamers; he left at dawn like a thief, with his fear of collective moving. Then the fat painter moved, pulled heavily and slowly because his barge was the heaviest. He owned a piano and huge canvases, heavier than coal. His leaving left a vast hole in the alignment of barges, like a tooth missing. The fishermen crowded in this open space to fish and rejoiced. They had been wishing us away, and I believe it was their prayers which were heard rather than ours, for soon the letters from the police became more insistent.

I was the last one left, still believing I would be allowed to stay. Every morning I went to see the chief of police. I always believed an exception would be made for me, that laws and regulations broke down for me. I don't know why except that I had seen it happen very often. The chief of police was extremely hospitable; he permitted me to sit in his office for hours and gave me pamphlets to pass the time. I became versed in the history of the Seine. I knew the number of sunken barges, collided Sunday tourist steamboats, of people saved from suicide by the river police. But the law remained adamant, and the advice of the chief of police, on the sly, was for me to take my houseboat to a repair yard near Paris where I could have a few repairs made while waiting for permission to return. The yard being near Paris, I made arrangements for a tugboat to come for me in the middle of the day.

The tugboat's approach to the barge was very much like a courtship, made with great care and many cork protectors. The tugboat knew the fragility of these discarded barges converted into houseboats. The wife of the tugboat captain was cooking lunch while the manoeuvres were carried out. The sailors were untying the ropes, one was stoking the fire. When the tugboat and the barge were tied together like twins, the captain lifted the gang plank, opened his bottle of red wine, drank a very full gulp and gave orders for departure.

Now we were gliding along. I was running all over the houseboat, celebrating the strangest sensation I had ever known, this travelling along a river with all my possessions around me, my books, my diaries, my furniture, my pictures, my clothes in the closet. I leaned out of each little window to watch the landscape. I lay on the bed. It was a dream. It was a dream, this being a marine snail travelling with one's house all around one's neck.

A marine snail gliding through the familiar city. Only in a dream could I move so gently along with the small human heartbeat in rhythm with the tug tug heartbeat of the tugboat, and Paris unfolding, uncurling, in beautiful undulations.

The tugboat pulled its smokestacks down to pass under the first bridge. The captain's wife was serving lunch on deck. Then I discovered with anxiety that the barge was taking in water. It had already seeped through the floor. I began to work the pumps, but could not keep abreast of the leaks. Then I filled pails, pots and pans, and still I could not control the water, so I called out to the captain. He laughed. He said: 'We'll have to slow down a bit.' And he did.

The dream rolled on again. We passed under a second bridge with the tugboat bowing down like a salute, passed all the houses I had lived in. From so many of these windows I had looked with envy and sadness at the flowing river and passing barges. Today I was free, and travelling with my bed and my books. I was dreaming and flowing along with the river, pouring water out with pails, but this was a dream and I was free.

Now it was raining. I smelled the captain's lunch and I picked up a banana. The captain shouted: 'Go on deck and say where it is you want to stop.'

I sat on deck under an umbrella, eating the banana, and watching the course of the voyage. We were out of Paris, in that part of the Seine where the Parisians swim and canoe. We were travelling past the Bois de Boulogne, through the exclusive region where only the small yachts were allowed to anchor. We passed another bridge, and reached a factory section. Discarded barges were lying on the edge of the water. The boat yard was an old barge surrounded with rotting skeletons of barges, piles of wood, rusty anchors, and pierced water tanks. One barge was turned upside-down, and the windows hung half wrenched on the side.

We were towed alongside and told to tie up against the guardian barge, that the old man and woman would watch mine until the boss came to see what repairing had to be done.

My Noah's Ark had arrived safely, but I felt as if I were bringing an old horse to the slaughterhouse.

The old man and woman who were the keepers of this cemetery had turned their cabin into a complete concierge's lodge to remind themselves of their ancient bourgeois splendour: an oil lamp, a tile stove, elaborate sideboards, lace on the back of the chairs, fringes and tassels on the curtains, a Swiss clock, many photographs, bric-à-brac, all the tokens of their former life on earth.

Every now and then the police came to see if the roof was done. The truth was that the more pieces of tin and wood the boss nailed to the roof, the more the rain came in. It fell on my dresses and trickled into my shoes and books. The policeman was invited to witness this because he suspected the length of my stay.

Meanwhile the King of England had returned home, but no law was made to permit our return. The one-eyed man made a daring entry back and was expelled the very next day. The fat painter returned to his spot before the Gare d'Orsay – his brother was a deputy.

So passed the barge into exile.

Illustration by Jean Cocteau, from his novel *The Miscreant*

Colette

COLETTE was born at Saint-Sauveur-en-Puisaye in Burgundy in 1873. She married Henri Gauthier-Villars when she was twenty, who ran a factory of ghost-writers in Paris and compelled Colette to write 'spicy' fiction. He introduced her to the Paris demi-monde, and she collaborated with him on the 'Claudine' books published under his *nom de plume*, Willy. He was, however, an excellent editor, and from him she learned much about the craft of writing. She finally broke away and obtained a divorce, after which she became a music-hall performer; her experiences of this period provided a backdrop for *La Vagabonde* and *L'Envers du Music-Hall*. Her second marriage was to Baron Henri de Jouvenel, editor of the newspaper *Le Matin*. Their daughter, Colette de Jouvenel, Colette's only child, was born in 1913. She was at her most productive from the 1920s to the 1940s, during which time she wrote her most celebrated works, including *Chérie*, *La Fin de Chérie*, *Gigi* and *Duo*. At the age of sixty-two Colette married the writer Maurice Goudeket. At the time of her death in Paris in 1954 she had published over fifty books and was, unquestionably, the foremost woman writer in France of the first half of the twentieth century.

'Colette wrote about "those pleasures which are, lightly, called physical". She never deserts the world of sense in her writing. She is, of all prose writers, the most responsive to the natural world. No writer can make you hungrier for whatever may be touched, seen, smelled, tasted, heard. She is alive to the joys, pains, vagaries of love; she condemns nothing but cruelty, and understands even dishonesty.' – Allan Massie, *Sunday Telegraph*

The Bracelet *and* The Victim

These two stories are taken from the collection *The Other Woman,* first published by Peter Owen in 1971.

The Bracelet

'. . . TWENTY-SEVEN, twenty-eight, twenty-nine . . . There really are twenty-nine . . .'

In mechanical fashion Madame Angelier counted and re-counted the little rows of diamonds. Twenty-nine brilliant, square diamonds, set in a bracelet, sliding coldly like a thin, supple snake between her fingers. Very white, not very big, admirably well matched – a real connoisseur's piece. She fastened it round her wrist and made it sparkle under the electric candles; a hundred tiny rainbows, ablaze with colour, danced on the white table-cloth. But Madame Angelier looked more closely at the other bracelet, three finely engraved wrinkles which encircled her wrist above the brilliant snake.

'Poor François . . . If we're both still here, what will he give me next year?'

François Angelier was a businessman travelling in Algeria at the time but, present or absent, his gift marked the end of the year and the anniversary of their wedding. Twenty-eight pieces of green jade, last year; the year before, twenty-seven plaques of old enamel mounted on a belt . . .

'And the twenty-six little Dresden plates . . . And the twenty-five metres of old Alençon lace . . .' With a slight effort of memory Madame Angelier could have gone as far back as the four modest sets of knives and forks, the three pairs of silk stockings.

'We weren't rich, just then . . . Poor François, how he has always spoiled me . . .' She called him, within her secret self, 'poor

François', because she felt guilty about not loving him enough, failing to appreciate the power of affectionate habit and enduring fidelity.

Madame Angelier raised her hand, crooked her little finger upwards, extended her wrist in order to erase the bracelet of wrinkles, and repeated with concentration, 'How pretty it is . . . How clear the diamonds are . . . How pleased I am . . .' Then she let fall her hand and admitted that she was already tired of the brand-new piece of jewellery.

'But I'm not ungrateful,' she sighed naïvely. Her bored glance wandered from the flowered table-cloth to the sparkling window. The smell of Calville apples in a silver basket made her feel slightly sick and she left the dining-room.

In her boudoir she opened the steel case which contained her jewellery and decked out her left hand in honour of the new bracelet. The ring finger had a ring of black onyx, a brilliant tinged with blue; over the little finger, which was delicate, pale and slightly wrinkled, Madame Angelier slipped a hoop of dark sapphires. Her prematurely white hair, which she did not dye, looked whiter when she fixed into its light curls a narrow little band sprinkled with a dust of diamonds, but she removed the ornament at once.

'I don't know what's the matter with me. I'm not in form. It's tedious being fifty, in fact . . .'

She felt uneasy, greedy, but not hungry, like a convalescent whose appetite has not yet been restored by the fresh air.

'Actually, is a diamond as pretty as all that?'

Madame Angelier yearned for visual pleasure combined with the pleasure of taste; the unexpected sight of a lemon, the unbearable squeak of the knife which cuts it in two, makes one's mouth water with desire.

'I don't want a lemon. But the nameless pleasure which escapes me, it exists, I know it, I remember it! So, the blue glass bracelet . . .'

A shudder contracted Madame Angelier's relaxed cheeks. A

miracle, the duration of which she could not measure, allowed her, for the second time, the moment she had lived through forty years earlier, the incomparable moment when she looked in rapture at the light of day, the rainbow-coloured and misshapen image of objects through a piece of blue glass, bent into a circle, which had just been given to her. That piece of glass, which might have come from the East and was broken a few hours later, had contained a new universe, shapes that dreaming did not invent, slow, serpentine animals which moved in pairs, lamps, rays congealed in an atmosphere of indescribable blue . . .

The miracle ended and Madame Angelier, feeling bruised, was thrown back into the present and the real.

But from the next day she went from antique dealers to bargain basements, from bargain basements to glassware shops, looking for a glass bracelet of a certain blue. She did so with the passion of a collector, the care and dissimulation of a crank. She ventured into what she called 'impossible districts', left her car at the corner of strange streets and in the end, for a few centimes, found a hoop of blue glass that she recognized in the darkness, bought mutteringly and took away.

By the suitably adjusted shade of her favourite lamp, on the dark background of old velvet, she put down the bracelet, bent over it, awaited the shock . . . But she saw only a circle of bluish glass, an ornament for a child or a savage, moulded hastily, full of bubbles; an object whose colour and material she recalled; but the powerful and sensuous genie who creates and feeds the visions of childhood, who dies mysteriously within us, progressively disappearing, did not stir.

With resignation Madame Angelier realized in this way her true age and measured the infinite plain over which there moved a being for ever detached from herself, inaccessible, foreign, turning away from her, free and rebellious even to the command of memory: a little girl of ten wearing round her wrist a bracelet of blue glass.

The Victim

FOR THE FIRST twelve months of the war it had been a daily struggle, for her and for us, to keep her alive, a kind of bitter game, or challenge to evil destiny. She was so pretty that all she need have done for a living, my goodness, was to sit back. But it was precisely this beauty, and then her situation as a young woman who had had her 'friend' killed in 1914, that filled us with compassion. We hoped to keep her fragile halo for her and during her widowhood give her first of all food and then that luxury: chastity.

This was a more difficult task than one might have thought, for we were dealing with the strangely fine feelings of an emotional suburban girl who was an honest businesswoman. Josette agreed that everything can be bought and sold, even a disgusted breast, even an insensitive mouth. But a gift pure and simple made her suddenly angry and flushed with wounded pride: 'No, thank you . . . I don't need it . . . No, we don't agree about the little bill for the jacket. I owed you fifty sous from last week . . .'

In order to prevent her from fading away or returning gloomily to a trade which disgusted her in advance we were obliged to make her sew, iron and cover lampshades. She only wanted to work in her own place, miles away, in a 'bedroom with boxroom', furnished mainly with photographs, where beneath a dismal, hygienic smell of coarse soap hung the distinctive perfume of a dark-haired girl with white skin.

During the winter of 1914 she would arrive gaily, bringing her work: 'It's me! Don't let me disturb you!'

A toque, or some sort of hat, a narrow skirt which restricted her impatient steps, boots which had been turned inside-out and remade – for her little feet swam ironically in our shoes – and the rusty fur necklet that she preferred – it was more 'chic'! – to the coat that one of us had offered. And gloves! – but naturally! but always! – gloves. Her smooth beauty overcame this poverty. I've never encountered anything smoother than this child, whose black hair was never curled or waved, arranged artistically over smooth temples, and gleaming like valuable wood anointed with fine oil. Her pure, slightly prominent eyes, the supple cheeks, the mouth and chin seemed to tell everyone 'See how attractive we can be with the minimum of curliness.'

'I've brought back your little skirt,' explained Josette. 'I haven't edged the hem, it would have been stronger but it would have looked common. Just because there's a war on is no excuse for looking common, is it? And the blouse you wanted me to cut out of the evening coat, do you know what I found when I unpicked it? A hem turned in as much as that! Enough to make a big sailor collar to match!'

She shone with delight at being self-employed, at paying her way, at not being any liability. She had always 'had lunch before coming', and we used subterfuges to make her take away half a pound of chocolate.

'Josette, someone gave me this chocolate, I'm suspicious of it, it must be some drug . . . Be a dear, try it, then tell me if it made you ill . . .'

She accepted a sack of coal from Pierre Wolff, because I had told her that the playwright had noticed her when she was an extra at the Folies and still found the memory exciting.

She hardly ever spoke about her 'friend', an obscure actor who had been killed by the enemy. But sometimes she looked at the pictures in the illustrated magazines of 1913: 'Do you remember that revue? It was well staged, there isn't any . . . And who'd believe my luck? The author was going to give me a small part in his next revue! It's a long way off, his next revue!'

One theatre half opened its doors, two theatres, ten theatres, and cinemas. Josette couldn't keep still.

'The Gobelins, the Montrouge and the Montparnasse are going to put on a season of plays, did you know? And then, the Moncey wants to put on a season of operetta, and the Levallois too . . . The only thing, the thing that really matters, is to know whether the artists will be able to get the Metro home afterwards. At Levallois there won't be any Metro or tram, naturally . . .'

She disappeared for three weeks and came back thinner, suffering from a cold, and proud of herself: 'I've got an engagement, Madame! *Miss Helyett* three times a week, I'll play one of the guides and possibly another small part too! Three times a week, and twice on Sundays!'

'How much will you get?'

She looked down.

'Oh, you know, they're taking advantage of the war . . . I get three francs fifty for each performance. The other days, naturally, we aren't paid . . . And the show changes every fortnight, so we have to rehearse every day . . . That's why I haven't had time to finish the little cami-knickers . . .'

'There's no hurry . . . And how do you get home in the evenings?'

She laughed.

'Shanks's pony, naturally. An hour and a half's walk, I'll wear out more shoes than tyres. But they've told me that I might possibly have a part in *Les Mousquetaires au couvent* . . .'

How could we keep her back? She radiated freedom, zest, fatigue, and theatrical fever . . . She went away, for months . . .

In August 1916 I was buying a child's toy at one of those charity bazaars where they sell packets of coffee, necklaces of dyed wooden beads, raffia baskets and woollen things, and I was waiting for an elegant customer to leave me a space at the counter.

'That, that, yes, the blue jumper, and then the four bags of coffee,' she said. 'That will make us four separate parcels for the front, I'll write the addresses for you, Mademoiselle. I'll take the little baskets with me in my car . . .'

'In your car, Josette!'

'Oh, Madame, what a surprise! It's you I'm going to take in my car – yes, yes, I am, just for a moment, just the time to take you home . . .'

She had not warned me that 'her' car already contained a well-turned-out man with barely greying hair, and she ordered him to unfasten one of the spare seats, for himself. She sat next to me and talked, trying to give the impression that she had forgotten the man's presence. He looked at her like a slave, but Josette's black eyes did not look at him even once. She removed one of her gloves and revealed scintillating rings; the man seized this fluttering hand and gave it a long kiss. She did not withdraw it but closed her eyes and only opened them again when he had raised his head. After a short silence the motor car reached my house and Josette issued instructions to the man: 'Get out, then, you can see your seat's in the way. Madame can't get by.'

He obeyed at once, made his excuses and Josette, as she left me, promised she would come to see me: 'As soon as the rehearsals at the Edouard VII are over, I'll be there.'

She came a few days later, all in lawn and 'summer furs', a string of pearls round her neck and carrying a moiré handbag covered with brilliants. But she had not changed her coiffure in any way, and her unwaved, uncurled hair still lay flat over her temples as though she were a Japanese child.

'My little Josette, I don't need to ask what's happened to you . . .'

She shook her head. 'Every misfortune, naturally! I've joined the ranks of the *nouveaux riches*.'

'So it seems. Are you in haricot beans or projectiles?'

'I'm in nothing – him . . . oh, he can buy or sell whatever he likes – the thing is, he doesn't interest me.'

'Now listen, for a military supplier he's very nice.'

'Yes, he's very nice. It's true all the same that he's very nice.'

She contemplated without seeing them her beautiful white suede shoes, and her face, although illuminated by pearls, snow-white lawn, pale fur and silk, seemed to have lost its glow.

'If I understand you correctly, Josette, you regret the time when . . .'

'Not at all,' she interrupted sharply. 'Don't imagine that! Why should I regret a time when I was cold, when I didn't have enough to eat, when I ran about in mud and snow, when without you and those other ladies I would have fallen ill or worse? Not at all! I belong to my country, I like what's good. Now that I no longer have anyone at the front except a few friends I look after in memory of Paul, why shouldn't I be the lady with the motor car and the necklace, instead of the tenant downstairs? Fair's fair. By doing what I do I think I'm worth the blue fox furs and the tulle underwear. . . . That's certainly the least of it, since as far as that man's concerned, the man you saw, I'm the victim!'

I said nothing. Sensitively, she felt that these words were creating a gulf between us.

'Madame, Madame,' she exclaimed, 'you don't know. You're blaming me . . . I swear to you, Madame . . .'

She nearly burst into tears and took a grip on herself.

'Madame, you've seen that man. You don't have to have second sight to understand that there's no better man than he is. Madame, he's good. Madame, he's sensitive, and well groomed, he's everything – which doesn't stop me from being the victim.'

'But why, my child?'

'Why? But quite simply because I don't love him, and I'll never love him, Madame. If he were ugly and revolting and stingy, I'd console myself, I'd tell myself: "It's quite natural that I can't bear the sight of him. He's bought me, I hate him, it's quite normal." But, Madame, that man, I don't love him because I don't love him, oh my goodness, how unhappy I'm making myself because of him . . .'

She was silent a moment, searching for words, examples. 'Now look, the day before yesterday he gave me this ring. And so nicely! Then, I began to cry . . . He called me "My sensitive little girl!" and I cried thinking of the pleasure I'd have felt on receiving a ring from someone I loved, and I was angry with him, I was so angry with him I could have bitten him . . .!'

'What a child you are, Josette . . .'

She struck the arm of the chair in irritation.

'No, Madame, you're wrong, forgive me! One is not such a

child as that, in Paris, at twenty-five. I know what love is, I've
been through it. I have a very loving nature, although it doesn't
show. The result is I consider myself the victim of that man, and
I'm jealous of him, so jealous it makes me ill.'

'Jealous?'

'Yes, envious. I envy everything he has, and which I can't have,
for he's in love. The other day the little Peloux girl said to me at
rehearsal, "Your friend has a nice mouth, he must kiss well." "I've
no idea," I replied. And it's true that I've no idea, I shan't know.
The woman who finds him attractive will know. I shall die without knowing whether he kisses well or badly, if he makes love well
or badly. When he kisses me my mouth becomes like . . . like nothing. It's dead, it feels nothing. My body too. But as for him, the
little I give him – you should see his face, his eyes. Ah, he gets a
thousand times more from it than I do! Ten thousand times more!

'Then you can imagine, one's nerves . . . Sometimes I'm
unkind, I take my revenge, I'm sharp with him. Once I was so
unkind that he wept. That was the last straw! If I'd said another
word I'd have gone too far. The trouble is that I know what it's
like to have someone in your life who's only to say one word to
make you feel in heaven or hell. I'm that someone for him. He has
everything, Madame, he has everything! And he can't do a single
thing for me, Madame, not a thing – he can't even make me
unhappy!'

She began to sob and her words came through her violent
tears. 'Tell me, Madame, am I wrong, tell me?' But I couldn't find
anything – and I haven't found anything since – to say to her.

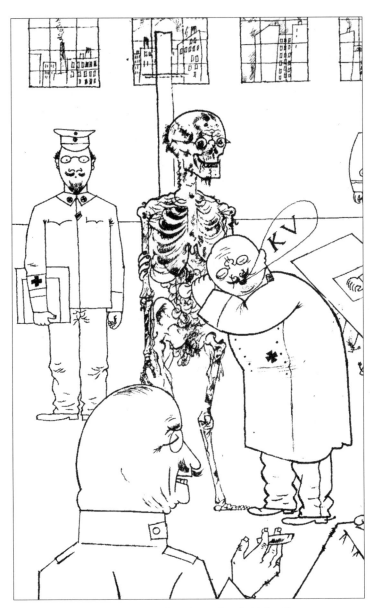

Fit For Active Service by George Grosz, from *George Grosz* by Herbert Buttner

Cesare Pavese

CESARE PAVESE was born in the Piedmont in 1908. Now considered one of Italy's pre-eminent writers, he was unable to publish his creative writing during the fascist era and instead channelled his energies into translating the work of English-language authors into Italian. His particular field of interest was twentieth-century American authors – notably Sherwood Anderson, Gertrude Stein, John Steinbeck, John Dos Passos, Ernest Hemingway and William Faulkner – however, he was greatly influenced by Herman Melville as well as the Irish writer James Joyce. He was incarcerated by the Mussolini government in 1935 – inspiring his novel *The Political Prisoner* – and lived with the partisans between 1943 and 1945. The bulk of his work – stories, poems and novels, such as *The Moon and the Bonfire* and *Among Women Only* – appeared between 1945 and his suicide in 1951.

'A very great writer. Pavese, Camus, Forster are the most liberal of the great writers of the twentieth century.' – *Spectator*

Fag-End Blues

This story is taken from the collection *Told in Confidence*, first published
by Peter Owen in 1971.

MASINO – OTHERWISE KNOWN as Tommaso Ferrero – had a job
with a Turin newspaper that he found completely satisfying. In all
fairness, though, I should add that it's easy enough to feel satisfied
with working as a journalist at Masino's age – he was twenty-four
or twenty-five – especially since he had a highly sensitive aware-
ness of what would interest the public. I'm not talking now of his
more intimate personal affairs – quite a different matter. Speaking
generally, I should point out that his work as a reporter, a mild
form of torture for any mentally active young man, left him almost
the whole morning free for strolling round the town or staying
indoors, working or idling the time away, and primarily to enjoy
the spectacle of life as it wakes to a new day. I agree that Masino
was one of those bright, dashing young fellows who, probably
without even realizing it, can create for themselves a magnificent
way of living, full of adventure and a wide range of interests. The
best of it is that, to do so, they have no need to go outside the great
mechanical structure of life as it is today. In such a position, older,
more experienced men would find that all they could do is to
curse their lot and fret away their souls, mourning for bygone
days. Instead, we newspapermen just adapt ourselves like a pen-
dulum and keep happy. After all, that's the most important thing.

Masino, then, woke one morning full of energy and listened
with profound complacency to the noise of trams and motor cars
coming up to him through the open window, rising above the
pungent fumes in the street to his room that until then was full of
fresh air.

By this time, the people of the house were knocking at his door. They had taken it upon themselves to clean his room and make his bed *every morning*! After a brief exchange of greetings they clustered round him, pestering him to let them make a start. Being the kind of man he was, Masino yielded to this pressure, mentally linking his retreat with another great cosmic urge – a longing to plunge into water and try out his muscles. All the usual odds and ends of thought, impulses and ideas drifted through his mind, as they normally do in the morning. But there was something different about this particular day, something much more definite. Now and then Masino started to whistle, a sure sign that he was thinking out a way to make money. His plan was already clear in his head when, striding out briskly as if late for an urgent appointment, he swung through the doorway of his room, shouting to the whole house to let him get out and leave him in peace.

In due course there he was, back again, sitting at his little table in the freezing cold. The window was closed now, muffling the noise of the trams. A couple of books lay on the table, with a pile of printer's proofs, headed: Dramatic Performances and Stage Directions. Masino was smoking and thinking hard. He now knew exactly what he wanted to do. His idea, simple yet ambitious, was to write a happy song. Not for publication, nor to be circulated among his friends, but just to create a *canzonetta*. He felt a kind of physical necessity to satisfy this urge.

Masino was a bright lad and knew better than to imagine he could get up one morning and start writing poetry straight out of his head as if he were dashing off a thank-you letter. He already had a lyric in mind – a blend of adventure and light-hearted philosophy – but to bring these ideas to fruition is by no means easy and would be pointless anyway. No matter what Masino had in mind for his lyric, he had for some time been aware of a growing conviction (and was especially aware of it on that particular morning) that he was not the sort of man to live with a woman. This had nothing to do with having a wife and children, nor a mistress to waste his evenings with idle chatter and exchanging kisses. Masino knew what to do. Perhaps the root cause of his lack of interest was simply the fact that he viewed a lovely woman as someone to pass the time with, while the only woman who really matters to a man will bind him hand and foot. Then there's the nuisance of remaining faithful to her. Masino wanted nothing to do with that. Whether he was right or wrong in these ideas of his, in one respect they were well founded. He had never deceived himself about love. He was a cynic, as many people were after the war.

Masino had his own views about women. He was a native of Piedmont, and Piedmontese men keep themselves to themselves. Even now we don't know enough about them to understand. Their women folk must be either stupid or cunning. I can tell you that when a Piedmontese lad brings home a girl he wants to marry, the rest of the family at once do their best to drive her away by ridiculing her personally. So they lose her services which they could have had for nothing. That's the way things are in Piedmont.

Masino had not written a musical comedy since the war, because his ambition was to become known to the public as a more serious writer. The only thing he really loves is his birthplace, and he raises his glass to it every chance he gets.

To look at him, on the morning I'm talking about, sitting smoking in his room, humming to himself or whistling in his ear-splitting way, he certainly didn't seem to be harbouring a grudge against love, still less about life. Yet he had already written the title at the top of the first page: Fag-End Blues. 'Blues' means a melancholy song, as Masino knew well.

There he sat, smoking his last cigarette of the morning, gazing out of the window. The October mist had cleared by now, leaving a cloudless sky, bright and almost warm. On the table in front of him lay the theme song he had just finished for his blues. The refrain always has to be written first and Masino was enjoying giving it a final polish. Nothing is pleasanter than sitting smoking and revising one's practically finished work. Every now and then he glanced at it again. The words ran like this:

Throw away your fag-end. There are plenty more around.
Why stand staring down at it?
And if a faithless girl-friend plays you false,
Why worry? There are a hundred better ones around.
Cigarettes are to be used, then tossed aside.
It's the same with women. Don't wait to get your fingers burnt,
Or hang on to your fag-ends when there's nothing left to smoke.

By this time Masino's mood had changed. Now he felt an urge to move about, go somewhere, enjoy what life had to offer and express its significance in his *canzonetta*.

At last a thought struck him. At this time of day the Variety Café would be quiet. He could work there. He urgently needed a change of scene, so he quickly got ready, remembering vaguely that the café was a favourite haunt of singers and instrumentalists.

It's always easy enough to start anything, but bringing it to completion is the devil's own job, a maxim so well known that the mere mention of it seems too silly for words. That's what Masino had been trying to do, slaving away, cursing through his clenched teeth while his head felt fit to split, forcing himself to create, within the traditional limitation of a couplet, some story or other that could lead up to his *ritornello*.

There were no customers in the café just then. A white-coated bar attendant with a broad, wrinkled face was idly fiddling with the espresso coffee machine. Masino's brain was in such a whirl that he started humming over and over again the tune he had just written. Then he began talking to the attendant. 'How's the season going for you, this year?'

'The season? It doesn't make much difference to me. You're a song-writer, aren't you? Would you be willing to write songs in collaboration with another fellow?'

'That all depends.'

'Listen to me. I can put you in touch with a musician . . . A fellow from the South, maybe even from Tripoli. His name's Ciccio, and he wants to have someone write a great song for him. Somebody different from the ordinary song-writer, you know, better educated. You seem to me to be just the sort of man he wants. He's a well-known musician and plays wind instruments. He's written a lot of music, too . . . I don't remember what.'

'Do you make a lot at it, working together?'

'If I had to live on that income I'd really be in a mess.'

'This Ciccio of yours, does he come from Naples?'

'Go and ask him. Here he comes.'

The bar attendant was an observant man who noticed what anyone else might have missed – a gesture that called him over to the little table where Masino was sitting. Masino liked to be taken for an astute man of business, and with an air of engaging frankness he made a general comment or two. The barman did not reply and went back behind the counter, pausing on the way to rub a little tap with a duster he had in his hand. For a moment Masino felt too embarrassed to speak. The barman said no more and Masino hardly knew what to say himself. Then, uncertain of his ground, he asked: 'Anything to do with Ciccio's group in Naples?' The barman smiled but didn't reply.

The huge fellow who had just come in had sharp eyes almost buried in rolls of fat. He unbuttoned his long coat, then, puffing and blowing, threw himself into a chair at the first table he came to. 'Evening, all,' he said. 'Good health, everybody. I'll have my usual.'

Masino looked at him with considerable interest while the attendant worked the coffee machine. When the fat man had been served with his coffee he started talking. 'It happens all the time. No matter where I go, I always come across someone from Naples.'

'Sir,' said the barman, 'this is the gentleman I told you about. He's a composer who can perhaps help you with the song you have in mind.'

The musician looked at Masino and said good-humouredly,

'As soon as I came through the door I knew he was the man. Well, my lad, you've something to tell me, I gather.'

Masino stayed where he was, thinking to himself: 'If I don't watch out he'll make me look a fool.' The attendant turned away towards the bar counter and Masino found himself agreeing with Ciccio in general terms that popular contemporary art in the form of *canzonette* might be of some interest to him.

'*Canzonette*? You must be joking,' the maestro replied. 'We don't bother to write words for songs. That's a purely commercial affair. What I'm looking for is someone, a poet perhaps, who can write a superb song for me. An Italian song, of course. Are you a poet?'

'Yes, oh yes, but first we must reach a clear understanding as to the kind of song you have in mind. Words and music must be in complete accord, otherwise they can destroy each other, and the whole feeling of the song is lost.' Masino, trying to discuss the popular taste in music, felt he must sound an utter fool.

'What?' the fat man retorted. 'Of course I know the tune and the libretto must correspond, but they are two different things and can react against one another. Sentimentality, though, is concerned with only one thing, sentiment.'

'That's precisely what I had in mind,' Masino replied, irritated. 'We must have something modern that can express in popular form what people are thinking today. The music, too, must be in line with current trends.'

'I see what you mean,' the maestro declared thoughtfully. 'The song will not only be popular, it will also be artistic.' It might have been August from the way the maestro had to mop up his perspiration. Masino returned to his attack. 'Just as music has been brought up to date, the words must be those in current use today.'

'I'm not quite clear about that,' the maestro said, as if he was beginning to agree. Masino went on: 'The words are an embodiment of the tune, just as the music appeals to the soul. I'm thinking of words that correspond with the spirit of today's music.'

'A foxtrot is no longer romantic. Nor is a waltz or a blues. Take jazz, now. Have you written any words for a jazz tune? Who has the music score?'

Here Masino, shamefaced, had to confess he was new to the job. He half feared a furious outburst. It did not come. Instead, the maestro was delighted. 'You're fine. Certainly I'm no budding poet myself. The tune for the song needs very sensitive handling.'

Masino, true son of Piedmont, leaped to the defence of jazz. 'In that matter we must learn from America. Have you ever listened to music composed for a film?'

'Don't talk to me about sound films. They're reducing our musicians to starvation. America? America? We're the ones who made America. We're all Naples men down there. What do you expect? We're the best in the world when it comes to composing melodies.'

Masino had it on the tip of his tongue to retort that Italy was not America, but he reflected that first of all he would he supplied with the tap-dancing rhythm or what passed for it. Gossip in the café suggested that even Turin wasn't certain how jazz would develop.

'In any case, sir, you'll want to see what I can do before you decide to work with me, won't you?'

'That's a good idea. Come and see me in my lodgings, though I haven't got a piano down there.'

'Yes, but I must prepare something for you, surely. What do you suggest?'

'My lad, if you want to work with me, the first thing you must have is inspiration. That's up to you. Do what you think best. Once I hear it and like it, then we can get down to business.'

'Maestro, you must give me an exhibition of your own musical skill, if we are to understand each other.'

'My music? I leave it all to a deputy, a man of straw. My real job is composing popular tunes. D'you know the successful "Our Very Own Tango"? That's one of mine.'

*

Early in the afternoon Masino was waiting at a street corner – an occupation he had not foreseen that morning but one that had its part to play in the only adventure that had come his way that day. He had received a letter, ungrammatical but in a handwriting he knew, and he arrived promptly at the rendezvous specified in that letter. And here it's no good puzzling ourselves that Masino found it a bore to be going out with a pretty girl. Whatever kind of man he was, and no matter that he considered himself an enemy of all women, he could not resist the temptation to experiment and foster his very real hatred for them. It has been said that hate and love are akin, and in point of fact Masino, the champion, behaved as if he did not hate them at all. On that particular day Masino felt stupid and an arrant coward. Most men are a bit like that, and Masino certainly was.

The girl came along, only five minutes late. She was fairly well dressed for a clerk, which she was. They walked away together, he looking quite smart, she wearing a light brown coat and a little felt hat. As they met they shook hands cordially.

'How are things going for you, baby?'

'OK. I'm all right. Glad you could manage to come.'

'As you see.'

They sheltered under a porch, and Masino asked how she had been able to get away at such short notice.

'I was all by myself and feeling lonely,' she said. 'There's no one to keep an eye on us at the office. Thank you for coming, darling.'

Masino very much disliked that mode of address and had told her so several times, but the girl used it on purpose to tease him, smiling as she did so. This time Masino decided to overlook it.

'Well, Daina, where shall we go?'

'I don't know. Anywhere you like.' She was called Daina, but Masino made a practice of giving people pet names, as a sign of possession, a word she could base all sorts of fancies upon, when he was not with her. He changed it from Daina to Dina then to Dinah, spelt the English way. So much the better. One cannot always succeed.

'It's odd, Daina, don't you think, that we meet only once every now and then, for a day or two, and then go for months without seeing one another again. D'you remember the last time? That meadow?'

Dina did remember. She bent her head with an uncertain smile and cuddled up closer to Masino's side. 'Let's go there,' she said to her companion. 'And that time on the boat. Isn't that worth mentioning? On that evening we nearly fell into the Po!'

After a short silence Masino came out with: 'Tell me then. What have you been doing to amuse yourself since we last met? All alone?' he added with a furtive little smile.

'Yes, I've been alone all the time. I hardly ever go out at all. Just once with that engineer, after that nothing.'

'You never really told me about that engineer, Daina. How did it turn out? All right?'

'How did you expect it to turn out? . . . Where are we going now?'

'I'm taking you to a fine place I know of, Daina. Shut your eyes and tell me about that engineer . . .'

'Well then, he had a car. Once he made me get into it and took me for a ride to the hills.'

'And what did you do when you got there?' Masino enquired shrewdly. Actually, apart from sweet talk, there was nothing linking Masino and Daina except the memory of sexual inter-course once or twice, plus a little friendliness not clearly defined. But on this particular day Masino felt, as it were, a nos-talgia for those brief experiences and wanted to hear all about that engineer, not out of jealousy but because it might be a good subject for starting a fierce argument later on. (Young people know all about that.)

Dina, very much surprised, told him: 'But it was nothing at all, dear.' Then, in a penitent tone, giving him a little smile, she went on: 'Not even what I did with you.'

'Thanks for telling me, Dina,' Masino started to say, but just then, as if to preserve his last shreds of dignity, a car almost knocked them down as they came out from the portico and broke the thread of his thoughts.

Dina said to him: 'Truthfully, I was always left alone. Sometimes I cried about it.'

'Ho, ho,' Masino laughed. 'You'd better find someone to marry you, my dear.'

For Dina this was no laughing matter. There was no one about in the street they were in at that moment, and Masino took advantage of the chance to give her a kiss, passionate but impersonal, caring nothing for the possibility that someone might come along. It was her spontaneous response to such kisses that had attracted Masino to her in the first place. He gave her another kiss or two, then they strolled on hand in hand. Dina paused a moment to shake out her coat, then gave a thought to her make-up. Masino held the mirror for her, realizing that she was really upset.

'Who do you suggest I should marry? So far the men I've met have all been in a good position, you, for instance, and that engineer. I couldn't bring myself to live with anyone in my own class, so who can I marry?' She was speaking slowly, breaking off to powder her face and touch up her lips. She sounded annoyed, rather than sorry, as she went on, 'So who can I marry? A workman? A labourer? A bricklayer? Then what? What sort of life should I have? I couldn't live with a factory-hand, either. He might knock me about. We'd never get on together. I simply couldn't.'

'I didn't suggest you should marry a workman,' Masino just managed to get a word in. 'The world's full of people. You never know who you might come across.' Without getting involved himself, Masino wanted his words to convey a certain meaning, but felt he was making a fool of himself. The fine self-confidence he had been conscious of at the start of the afternoon had vanished.

Without realizing it, Dina gave him a lead. 'I want to tell you something that happened to me. I've never said a word about it before. You know the fellow who waved at me, that Sunday when you took me out in a boat? He has a friend with piles of money, and another pal like himself. They go everywhere together and get up to all sorts of tricks. I happened to meet them in the street one day and the four of us went to a café. One of the fellows kept talking to the millionaire and the other told me their friend was frightfully rich, but a fool who had never yet made love to a woman. He suggested that if I were to fall in love with him it would be a fine thing for the three of us. Then they invited me up to their bachelor flat. The rich man came close behind me but he was too shy to say a word.

'The other two were busy around the flat, arranging every-thing, offering us tea and pastries. I chattered away, laughing gaily. After a while the fellow we saw in the boat started throwing his arms around me and kissing me. He wanted to undress me, but I wouldn't let him. Then two of them tried to persuade me and began threatening me. The rich one said nothing, so I ran over to him for protection, acting like a very determined woman, so he let me go.

'Well, I saw the other two men one day and they tried to walk along beside me, to keep me company they said. I didn't want them so they called me a fool. After all, I could just as well have got the millionaire to marry me, couldn't I? I could marry if I wanted to, but I don't. I was thinking if only I could find the right man . . .'

Masino was listening. He wouldn't have wanted to say so, but the idea of Dina being made to strip in that room upset him for the moment and he tried to put his feeling into words: 'They are nothing but a couple of dangerous rogues, stupid too. That's no way to behave, Dina, is it?' he said with a smile. 'But getting a bit of fun out of life is a different matter. Don't you agree?' He tried to smile at her again.

Dina smiled in response, but she looked pale and clung more closely to his arm. Neither spoke for a little while as they stood in a close embrace.

'Come with me tonight, Dina. Will you? I know a fine place to take you.'

'Where?'

Masino tried to find the right words. 'Let's have a while alone together. You'd like that, wouldn't you? Just like that time in the boat.' He hugged her even more tightly.

'Not today, Masino. I don't want to. Let's go somewhere together. Let's go to the cinema.'

'Why? We haven't seen each other for such a long time. Come on.'

'No, Masino. I don't want to. Let's behave ourselves.'

'Why? Is there any reason why not?' His smile had a double meaning.

'No. There's nothing to stop us. It's just that I'm not in the mood. Let's have a long chat instead. It's ages since we've seen each other.'

'We can talk there. We'd be quite alone together.'

'Afterwards we mightn't meet again for a long time. It's no good, not today.'

'Come on, Dina. Be a good sport. Come along.'

'No, Masino.' Her voice was firm now. 'I'd rather go home right away.'

Masino had to accept the fact that there was nothing doing, that day. Dina was determined to be let off. His anger almost choked him, but he managed to control it. Earlier, on his way to meet her, he considered making love to her as a matter of no importance, but by now his desires had multiplied. She had turned him down out of caprice. Simply a caprice. It annoyed him.

'Go home, then,' he retorted, starting to walk away. 'Go and find some other man to screw you.'

For a moment Dina stood perfectly still, then gave a sigh that was almost a groan and walked away so quickly she was almost running.

Masino had written his verses and was now sitting in the café smoking and waiting for Ciccio. By now the maestro had agreed, after a good deal of argument, to accept Masino's suggestion of using modern language in his *canzonette,* his blues. His fixed idea of what a song should be turned out to be merely a fixed idea that had entered his sensitive spirit to set right the evils of life in general.

With his masterpiece in his pocket, Masino sat there waiting. Meanwhile his verses were running through his mind as if they were spoken aloud. The first one was pretty well typical of all the others.

Fag-End Blues

How many pretty young girls you see in the street
Who look like dreams of love.
But if, poor fool, you stop one of them
You'll soon get wind of her.

You can watch them, models of propriety,
So shy they run away around a corner
If a man so much as winks at them.
Almost before they start talking familiarly

They'll ask you, 'Give me a fag.'
Then follows the usual rigmarole you know about.
But to go through it all a second time,
That would be a crime.

Women are made that way. It can be delightful
To smoke a cigarette with one of them, kiss her on the lips
Or lower down. But soon you'll feel uneasy.
Push her away quickly.

Like a half-smoked fag-end, such women
Emit a beastly smell.
Be careful, then, for charity's sweet sake,
And do not fool yourself that this is love.

Masino had managed to get that far. At last the maestro came in. The two men greeted each other and began walking towards the private rooms.

'Well, my fine lad, have you been working?' Don Ciccio asked, seeing that Masino was feeling too embarrassed to speak first.

'I've had a go at the blues,' Masino replied, taking the sheet out of his pocket.

'We'll have a look at it later, later,' Ciccio told him. 'On the piano. Even a blues can be a suitable matter for artistry. We're practically there.'

God willing, they arrived and climbed the almost impossible stairs and finally found themselves in a large cold room full of a medley of unrelated objects. There was a bed, a pair of trousers hanging in mid air, a guitar on the wall, and mountains of musical scores everywhere. There were a few oleographs around the guitar.

'Make yourself comfortable,' the maestro began. 'It's rather chilly here in the afternoons.' Without saying more he sat down at the piano, puffing and blowing. 'Now then,' he went on, 'is your *canzonetta* ready? Give it to me. If it inspires me, the matter is settled.' He took the sheet Masino passed to him (rather nervously, to tell the truth). Don Ciccio turned towards the music-rest, put down the manuscript and looked at the keys. Then he began: '"Fag-End Blues"? Isn't that a trifle grotesque for a title? Oh well, even the grotesque has some value. Now we'll see.' He read it through impassively, touching the piano keys now and then. Once, at the start of the second verse there was a crease in the paper, and he called Masino over to decipher a blot. Masino was calmer now and master of himself. When he had read the lyric, Don Ciccio looked at the keys again and began to play a tarantella, completely absorbed in it.

'I intended this for a blues tune,' Masino interrupted, somewhat timidly.

'I know you did, of course,' said the other. 'But just now I'm thinking about the plot. It gives me the idea that the grotesque element may not be too strong. What's your opinion, my lad?'

Masino, thus taken unawares, hardly knew what to say. There was a short silence, then Ciccio went on: 'It's verging on the comic. You've worked well, my lad, but we'll have to change the idea. The public won't put up with this, you know. We're saying the woman is a serpent, she's poison, and so far that's allowed. You're quite right, you know, lad. She's treacherous. You can't believe a word she says, but all the men are chasing her. No husband or lover in the theatre would quarrel with that. I agree with you, you know . . . I'm not married. Picking up a woman is worse than picking up a cigarette end in the street. All she wants is money . . .'

By now Masino had lost all hope but still wanted to interrupt the maestro, even with a lie. 'That's just the point. We're talking of street women.'

'Really? In this? That's yes and no, my boy. A blues song must be sad. All women can make a man sad. We can call them serpents, poisoners and so on, but we can't say that about streetwalkers, my lad. Believe me, it simply can't be done.'

Masino, as we know, was humble by nature and a native of Piedmont too. He hadn't been bored by it all. He put his manuscript away with a philosophic air and stood up to go, but the maestro detained him to listen to a song he had written. It was supper time before he got away.

Masino was a conscientious fellow, and on his way home he thought over what he had written. Turning those lines over in his mind for the rest of the evening and all night, they now seemed to him worse and worse. He felt quite ashamed of having written them. Then he remembered how Dina had looked at him that afternoon, as though her very life depended on him. 'However could I have treated her like that,' he asked himself, a pointless question. Next morning Masino woke up and started working again, listening happily to the noise of the trams and motor cars in the street outside.

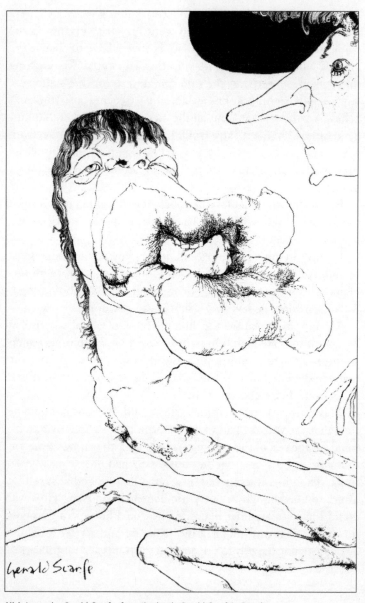

Mick Jagger by Gerald Scarfe, from the book *Gerald Scarfe's People*

Shusaku Endo

SHUSAKU ENDO was born in Tokyo in 1923. After the Second World War he studied in France until obliged to return to Japan because of ill health. He was the author of many books, and his novel *Silence* has been acclaimed as a masterpiece. Regarded as one of the great Japanese authors of the second half of the twentieth century, much of Endo's work features the conflict between east and west and in particular the history of Christianity in Japan, which was informed by his own Roman Catholic background. Several times shortlisted for the Nobel Prize, Endo won many other major literary prizes in his lifetime. His books have been translated into twenty-eight languages and include *The Sea and Poison*, *Wonderful Fool*, *Deep River*, *Scandal* and *The Samurai*. He died in Tokyo in 1996.

'Of all Japanese novelists, Shusaku Endo is the most accessible to Western readers . . . Saner than Mishima, closer to us than Kawabata and more universal than Tanizaki, Endo is one of the half-dozen leading novelists of the post-war period.' – Francis King, *Spectator*

Despicable Bastard

This story is taken from the collection *Stained Glass Elegies*, first published by Peter Owen in 1984.

'HEY, WHAT ARE you doing? You won't get away with that!'

He turned around in surprise. The supervisor they had nicknamed Centipede was standing behind him, hands thrust into the pockets of his work clothes.

'You may think you can slack off because nobody's looking, but I know what you're up to. I know!'

'I've got a headache.'

Egi, being a cowardly sort of person, blurted out the first excuse that came into his head.

He screwed up his face as though in pain and wiped his forehead with his hand, and strangely enough he began to believe that he actually did have a headache. The strength had gone out of his legs, and he staggered unsteadily.

The supervisor had walked on two or three steps when he turned around and studied Egi's movements with suspicious eyes. Then he came back and asked, 'Have you really got a fever?'

'Uh-huh,' Egi sighed.

'Then why didn't you say you were ill?' The supervisor knit his brows sullenly. 'You're hopeless. Go and report that you're leaving work early.'

Egi slipped out of the factory, avoiding the eyes of the other students. When he was outside, a sly smile appeared on his slender face. Caught up in the satisfaction of having eluded the normal eight hours of labour service and the pleasure of having outwitted his supervisor, he felt scarcely any guilt at leaving his classmates behind. He watched as a group of women from the volunteer corps, dressed in fatigues, came wearily towards him, dragging their shovels and straw baskets after digging an air-raid shelter. Even the sight of them did not fill him with the remorse of a deserter, and he went back to his dormitory in Shinano-machi.

The dormitory where Egi lived had been built by a Christian organization for the benefit of their members' children. Recently, however, many of the Christian students had been drafted or had otherwise withdrawn from the dorm, so unaffiliated students like Egi had been allowed to move in. Though it passed as a dormitory, the building was simply a brown-painted, two-storey wooden structure with no more than fifteen or sixteen rooms.

Egi realized that there would be nothing to do if he went back to his room, and that none of his dorm-mates would be back yet, so he made one of his rare visits to the Outer Gardens of the Meiji Shrine. He sat down on the grass and watched as a winter squall picked up scraps of straw and old newspapers and tossed them about. He extracted his aluminium lunch-pail from his knapsack, dejectedly took out the handful of rice that had been crammed into its corner, and slowly began to chew it.

As he worked his chopsticks, Egi thought vaguely about what would happen to him in the future. He had no idea what course the war would take. Of late he had not the slightest interest in whether Japan won or lost. His days were filled exclusively with hunger and the strain of having to work at a factory even though he was a student. It frightened him to think that one day he would be taken off to live in a barracks like so many of the senior students.

The winter sky was perpetually cloudy. From far in the distance he heard a dull roar, like the whirring of an aeroplane propeller. Two young nurses from the Keiō Hospital, laughing about something, came walking along the path at the edge of the lawn.

Egi set his lunch-box down and, thrusting his head forward like a baby tortoise, listened covetously to the nurses' sparkling voices. The laughter of young women, and the sight of white uniforms instead of work fatigues, seemed to have a freshness that was almost unbearable in contrast to his stifling daily existence.

'Hey!' A loud voice suddenly broke into Egi's thoughts. An NCO, dressed in a sweat-soaked military uniform with an armband reading 'Military Police', was standing in front of him, supporting his bicycle with his hand. 'Hey, what are you doing? Are you a student?'

Intimidated by the man's piercing gaze and the bony, square set of his jaw, Egi didn't reply. At the factory where he worked, there were often stories about military police catching and interrogating draft labourers and student workers who were shirking their duties.

'No answer, you bastard?' the officer said slowly. He leaned his bicycle against the trunk of a tree and, gripping his sword with his right hand, came up to Egi.

In a croaking voice Egi explained that he had left the factory early because of illness. 'I . . . I wasn't . . . wasn't . . . feeling well . . .' he stammered, his eyes fixed on the ground. But something in the way he stuttered gave the officer the impression that he was being mocked.

For an instant it felt to Egi as though his face had been hammered with a lead pipe. He cried out, covering his face with his hands.

'Make fun of me, will you, you bastard!' The officer began to kick Egi viciously. As the two nurses looked on in fear, Egi fell to his knees, his hands resting on the ground. The leather boots pounded into his knees and legs again and again.

'Forgive me, sir!' To quell the officer's wrath, Egi obsequiously employed military terminology. 'I am at fault. Please forgive me.'

The leather boots tramped off, but even after the bicycle had disappeared far down the road Egi remained motionless on his hands and knees. He glanced around in search of his glasses, which had been hurled to the ground; they lay in a clump of yellowed grass, their frames bent. When he spotted them, the first waves of searing humiliation surged up from the pit of his stomach. The nurses still stood watching apprehensively from behind a tree. 'Go away!' inwardly Egi pleaded with them. 'Please go away!'

He returned to the dorm, his legs throbbing. At the entrance, Iijima, a student from M. University, was removing his gaiters. Like Egi, Iijima was one of the students living at the dorm who was not a Christian. Egi was on the verge of telling him what had just happened to him, but, fearing that Iijima would despise him, he said nothing.

'I'm starving to death.' Finished with military drills for the day, Iijima massaged his feet. 'They're damned stingy with their food at this "Amen" dormitory.'

'Yeah,' Egi nodded feebly.

'You going to Gotemba?'

'Gotemba? What for?'

'Haven't you heard?' Iijima, a burly member of the university karate team, folded his arms. 'Next week they're going to a leper hospital called Aioi-en. It's supposed to be a regular event at this dorm. I imagine one of the "Amen" boys like Ōsono came up with the idea. But why should we have to go along when we aren't one of the "Amens"?'

Egi left Iijima sitting in the entranceway and went to his room, where he stretched out on his bed. His knees had started to ache. Gingerly, he pulled up his trousers to find that a good deal of skin had been scraped off. The gash was saturated with blood. Studying the wound, he was filled with a seething anger that a military policeman virtually his own age could be capable of such violence. Why hadn't he fought back? Why hadn't he put up a struggle? But he knew that he had no pride, that he was the sort of man who would abandon all principle in the face of violence or the threat of physical harm. 'It's like an act of nature,' he muttered to himself. 'The more you try to resist, the worse off you are.'

He dozed until sundown. From time to time he opened his

eyes a crack; the world outside the window was submerged beneath a grey evening haze. His room was cold, and his wounded knee hurt. He listened forlornly to the banging sounds from the next room, where Ōsono was shifting his desk around. Ōsono was a Christian, and had been at the dorm longer than anyone. He was a highly-strung, pallid-faced student at Tokyo University. And for some reason he seemed unable to rest unless he moved his desk to a new position every third day or so.

Egi finally woke up around dinner time. Favouring his swollen knee, he went downstairs to the cafeteria. The other students were silently eating the meagre helping of rice served to them in soup bowls. Ōsono stood by himself at the front of the room, reciting to the group from a history of the Japanese Christian martyrs. The founder of the dormitory had left instructions that the students were to say prayers each evening at dinner and that the student on duty that night was to read a passage from some religious work.

Like all the others, Egi ate with a sullen look on his face. Recently the students were too exhausted from days filled by military drill and labour service at the factory to find the energy or the enthusiasm to talk to one another during meals.

'In this torture the hands and feet of the prisoners were lashed together with ropes, which were tied behind their backs. They were then suspended from the ceiling while the officers beat them with whips.' In a strained voice, Ōsono was reading from what seemed to be an account of Christian martyrdoms in Hiroshima Prefecture at the beginning of the Meiji era.

But no one in the room had any interest in the story. The non-Christians were of course apathetic, but even the believers were only pretending to listen out of a sense of duty.

'Despite being subjected to this torture, neither Kan'emon nor Mohei nor any of the other Christians of Nakano village would agree to apostatize. In fact, calling upon the Holy Mother, they expressed their thanks to God for granting them this trial.'

At this point Ōsono slammed the book shut. Then with a

fraudulently pious gesture he crossed himself and dug into the soya beans and rice in his bowl. Egi stole a glance at Ōsono – that nervous face with the rimless glasses – and wondered if he was really interested in the sorts of things he had just been reading about. 'The whole book's a bunch of nonsense,' Iijima muttered from the next seat. Egi couldn't bring himself to agree, but it was obvious that every story Ōsono recited had to do with people who did not succumb to violence and torture. He recalled the blow to his face that afternoon, his entreaties as he knelt on the ground on all fours, his glasses knocked into the withered grass. He hated being so afraid of physical pain.

'You're lucky you weren't born into a Christian family. One blow and you'd chuck your God just like that!' Iijima called out to Egi in a loud voice. His remark was made half in jest, but no one laughed. Egi thought of the ugly scene that morning, and his face stiffened.

Late that evening Egi pulled out his hotplate, warmed up some dried cuttlefish he had been sent from home, and ravenously gobbled it up. Electric hotplates were banned in the dormitory because they often overloaded the fuses, but he had hidden one away in his cupboard for times of need. Concerned that the delicious smell of the cuttlefish might leak outside his door and attract the attention of the other starving students, he opened his window half-way and aired his room after cooking each fish.

Through the wall he heard Ōsono leaving his room. The door creaked and then slammed shut.

'Probably going to the toilet.' Egi relaxed and, stretching out on his bed, slowly relished the taste of the cuttlefish in his mouth. But this was imprudent. Ōsono thrust his pale face round the door, his rimless glasses glittering. When he recognized the aroma in the room, his eyes flashed and he peered sternly at Egi.

'It's cuttlefish,' Egi mumbled timidly, unable to endure Ōsono's accusing stare. 'My family sent it to me.'

Without a word Ōsono thrust a slice of the fish between his thin, colourless lips. 'Yeah. Next Sunday we're all going to put on a programme at the Aioi-en in Gotemba. The round trip will cost five yen. I thought I'd let you know in advance.' His eyes never strayed from the tentacles of the cuttlefish that still lay on the hotplate. 'As you're new to the dorm, this will be your first time. We do this programme every year.'

Ōsono explained that the Christian organization which had founded the dormitory also managed the Aioi-en leper hospital. For that reason the students at the dorm put on a show for the Gotemba clinic once every year.

'I know you're not a Christian, but, whether you are or not, you're a student at this dorm, so I knew you'd come along with us.'

'Is there anybody who isn't going?'

'That bastard . . . er, Iijima was reluctant at first, but he agreed to go after I told him I'd report him to the dorm supervisor.'

After Ōsono had left the room, Egi began to worry. He had no real knowledge about leprosy, but during his childhood he had been vaguely frightened of the disease. A beggar with twisted fingers had occasionally come begging with a frail voice around the streets of his village. Each time, his grandmother would quickly hide him in the linen closet. In his middle-school years he had passed through a period when he was virtually paranoid about the disease. This was the result of his reading an adult amusement magazine that featured photographs of gruesome skeletons and descriptions of the various symptoms of leprosy.

'It's supposed to be contagious if you have any kind of open wound on your body . . .' Gingerly, he pulled up his trouser leg. The injured knee, which he had just bandaged, felt hot and was beginning to swell. 'I wonder if I can beg off because of this,' he pondered aloud. On the other hand, he didn't like the thought of being called self-centred by Ōsono and the other Christians. 'If I go, I'll keep as far away from the patients as I can.'

As he made this resolution, Egi thought what a contemptible specimen of humanity he was. To visit a hospital and then try to avoid the patients out of a loathing for them – he knew full well how despicable that would be. But his fear of infection and his dread of physical pain still took precedence over everything else.

On Sunday morning Egi and the other students from the dormitory boarded the train for Gotemba at Tokyo Station. The train had arrived at the station only thirty minutes before, but already it was packed beyond capacity. Men dressed in patriotic uniforms with rucksacks on their laps, and women dressed in work pantaloons and carrying parcels of scavenged food had spread newspapers on the floor between the seats of the carriage and were jamming corridors.

On the platform one or two scraggy circles of patriots were croaking out military songs, but none of the passengers or the people scurrying along the platform paid the slightest attention to them. The dorm students were the only ones who paused at the door of the train to look at these ceremonies for recruits going off to the front. The thought crossed their minds that soon they too would stand on a station platform, their faces tense, while a circle of well-wishers clustered around them. Then, realizing that each of them was thinking the same thing, they abruptly lowered their eyes.

As they had left the dormitory and headed for the station, and now as they waited for the train to depart, the students had split into two groups – those who were Christians, and those like Iijima and Egi who were not. Sometimes the Christian students would glance back at Iijima, who had made his disapproval of this day-trip a matter of public record, and then whisper among themselves.

'Look at him now – Ōsono's enough to make you sick.' Iijima crouched down on the train step and spat loudly. Egi climbed on the step and looked down the platform. Ōsono had joined one of the groups surrounding a new recruit; he was clapping his hands and singing the war song. Seeing this hypocritical behaviour, Egi had to agree that Ōsono was something of a phoney.

When the packed train jerked to a start, Iijima again spat on to the tracks, then turned to Ōsono, who was standing beside him. 'It's a sorry fellow who has his circle and gets sent off to war only to come skulking right back, isn't it, Ōsono?' he asked lightly. His sarcasm was directed straight at Ōsono, who had been conscripted into a student division the previous year and been sent off with a great flurry, only to return ignominiously to the dormitory the very next day. Ōsono's nervous face turned red.

Leaning against the door to the lavatory, Egi tried to imagine the day when he would be given such a send-off. Life in boot camp would begin for him. Every day he would be beaten in the dark barracks room. At the thought of the pain his body would have to endure, Egi's chest constricted. Once again he thought of himself a week before, on his hands and knees in the Outer Garden, shamelessly pleading, 'I am at fault. Please forgive me.' 'That's just how it'll be if I end up in the army,' he thought. 'I'll gladly abandon all sense of self-esteem out of fear of being beaten. That's the kind of person I am.'

'Physical pain affects me more than mental torment,' he thought as his body swayed with the movement of the train. 'That's why I would abandon all pride and all conviction.'

Three hours later the train arrived in Gotemba. The sky was dark with clouds as they disembarked. Apparently word of their arrival time had been sent ahead; a middle-aged man dressed in a white smock was waiting beyond the ticket gate, a smile on his face.

'Welcome, welcome!' He bowed his head to the students, then identified himself as an officer worker at the Aioi-en. 'Our patients have been looking forward to this day for an entire month.'

The square in front of the station was deserted. Shops that had once sold souvenirs stood with their doors ajar, and not a sound could be heard from within. A single charcoal-burning bus awaited the group. It was held together with chewing-gum and spittle, the man explained with a smile. As they entered the bus, the odour of disinfectant stabbed at their noses.

When Egi smelled the disinfectant, the anxiety and fear, which had totally fled his mind, came flooding back. Perhaps a flock of patients had been sitting on these seats. Egi hurriedly covered his knee with his hand. The bus set off, rocking back and forth, and clattered along the streets. As it made its way along roads lined with pine trees, kicking up clouds of white dust, Egi began to be bothered by a pain in his knee that he had not noticed on the train. When he had checked the wound before leaving the dormitory that morning, a white layer of skin had begun to grow over it, but it still hadn't really begun to heal. It was possible that he might pick up some bacteria today at the Aioi-en. He looked apprehensively around the bus, noticing the cracked leather of the seats and the dust-coated windows.

Ōsono stood up in the aisle and suggested that the group sing a hymn. With a solemn look on his face, he raised his hand above his head and called, 'Ready – one, two, three.'

> 'O come all ye faithful,
> Joyful and triumphant,
> O come ye, O come ye to Bethlehem.
> Come and behold him,
> Born the king of angels.'

'Humph. Conceited slobs,' Iijima fumed from the seat behind Egi.

Egi turned round and whispered, 'Iijima, do you think we'll be all right?'

'Huh?'

'Do you think we'll get infected?'

'How should I know?' Iijima looked away. 'I can't stomach the zeal for charity they have at this dormitory.'

'How nice it would be if I could be as decisive about everything as Iijima is,' thought Egi. He looked vacantly out of the dusty window as farmhouses and fields whisked by. 'If it wasn't for this wound,' he told himself, 'even I could feel good about going to the hospital.'

He was disgusted with himself for being afraid of the patients at the Aioi-en. The same craven spirit that had impelled him to betray his own feelings and beg forgiveness from the MP a week earlier still had him in its grip. No matter how priggish and hypocritical Ōsono's attitude might be, the fellow had a strength he himself could never hope to emulate. He could not share Iijima's contempt for the Christian students.

The bus finally plodded its way out of the forest. In spite of the cloudy sky, faint rays from the afternoon sun had made the tree trunks glimmer a silver colour. There was no longer a house to be seen. The Aioi-en had been built in a region far away from any human settlements.

A wooden building with a red roof appeared beyond the trees. Two men dressed in white coats stood at the doorway waving their hands at the bus.

'Here we are!' called the staff worker, who was sitting next to the bus driver. They had arrived at the Aioi-en.

As he climbed off the bus, Egi looked about nervously to see if there were any patients walking around near him. But he could see no sign of anyone who might be a patient in the vicinity of the building.

Instinctively, Egi tried to stay close to Iijima. He felt more capable of making excuses and apologies for himself if he was with Iijima than if he mingled with the Christian students. But Iijima thrust his hands into the pockets of his tattered overcoat, spat on the ground and walked away from him.

The red-roofed building was the hospital's administrative office. In the reception room the students were given plates piled high with steamed potatoes and cups of muddy tea. They gnawed like dogs on the potatoes.

Smiling broadly, an old man dressed in a suit came into the room. 'Unfortunately our hospital director had to be in Shizuoka today. My name is Satō, and I work here in the office. Thank you all for coming.' Then, with one missing tooth leaving a gap in his smile, the chubby old man explained that the patients had been

136

eagerly awaiting this visit for over a month. 'Each one of our patients has saved a potato from their own rations to give to you.'

At this announcement, the students stopped chewing and the room fell silent.

'The patients have been waiting in the assembly hall for a half an hour already. They really are looking forward to your programme. Would you like to be disinfected before you go into the auditorium? I doubt whether anyone will be infected, but, well, you might feel more at ease.'

Egi and two or three others were about to get up from their chairs when Ōsono turned on them indignantly. 'If you have any regard for the goodwill these patients have shown us, you won't need disinfecting.'

'Well, well.' The old man seemed a little taken aback at Ōsono's agitation. 'Of course, the disinfecting really doesn't have much effect . . .'

There was a chilly silence. Egi stared in bewilderment at his trouser knee and at the plate of steamed potatoes. Then he raised his head and looked around for Iijima. His friend was standing with his arms folded, gazing petulantly at the ceiling.

'Well, shall we be going?' the old man said awkwardly.

Led by Satō and a young nurse, the students crossed the courtyard and headed towards the hospital building. The overcast sky seemed ready to release more rain at any moment. The infirmary was a long, narrow wooden structure of three storeys; with its peeling paint it looked very much like an old army barracks. To one side was a large playing field, possibly an exercise ground. Beyond this, fields of red earth, cultivated by the patients with only a mild case of the disease, stretched out beneath the slate-grey sky.

To Egi, it seemed a dark, depressing landscape. The patients suffering from Hansen's disease would never be able to leave this narrow space and venture into the world outside. Forsaken by their families and by society at large, they had no alternative but to die here. The thought filled Egi with an emotion somewhere between compassion and grief. But then his coat brushed against a wall of the infirmary and he quickly recoiled.

The auditorium was a hall large enough to accommodate about a hundred straw mats. It had a crudely constructed platform that served as a stage. Satō explained that the more able patients came here to listen to motivational lectures and to put on a monthly show.

'Last month they dramatized the dialogue between Jesus and Mary Magdalene,' the old man announced. 'Some of the patients are very good at that sort of thing. It was a great success.'

'We can't put on anything that impressive,' said Ōsono, blushing and nodding his head. 'But we'll do our best.'

The other students held their breath as they climbed the stairs to the dressing-room, which reeked of disinfectant. A black curtain hung between the stage door and the hall, so they could not get a glimpse of the assembled patients. But Egi estimated from the number of coughs and snorts that there must be about eighty patients waiting out there.

Anxiety gradually tightened its grip on Egi's chest. For whatever reason, since they had arrived here his wound had begun to ache more than ever. The thought that bacteria might already have got to him from somewhere made him even more resentful of Ōsono for refusing the disinfectant.

In the dressing-room, they heard a smattering of applause when Satō climbed on to the stage. Iijima located a tiny rip in the black curtain and peeped out at the audience, then turned to Egi with a sullen look.

'Look through here. There's swarms of them out there!'

There was more sparse applause, and Satō came back to the dressing-room. 'Well, it's all yours!'

As if they had planned it at some point, Ōsono led out about five of the Christian students and leaped up the stairs.

This time the applause was loud. When it ended, Ōsono gave the lead in his girlish voice, 'One, two, three.'

While the group sang hymns for the patients, the non-Christians listened in glum silence. Even if they had wanted to sing something just to spite Ōsono and his group, there weren't any songs that they all knew. It became evident that the Christian group had secretly been practising for some time in an effort to demonstrate something or other to the non-believers. When the chorus broke off, a literature student from Tokyo University named Hamada sang a German *lied*. Then in an excited voice Ōsono cried, 'I'd like to recite a poem for you all.' His voice trembled as he began.

> 'Life in this world is a path of pain.
> No matter what trials I encounter,
> Until the very moment of death . . .'

'A poem? Hah! He calls that a poem?' In exasperation Iijima opened the dressing-room window and spat. 'Is that supposed to cheer up the patients?'

Hesitantly, Egi brought his eye up to the hole in the curtain. And had his first look at the patients he feared so much.

The hall was dark, so he could not clearly distinguish the individual faces of the patients. Just as he had thought, the majority of them seemed to be middle-aged men. But as his eyes grew accustomed to the faint light, he noticed among the balding men several young women dressed in *meisen* silk kimonos or white aprons. They kept their hands on their laps and tilted their heads to listen to the performance. Egi looked towards the back of the auditorium. Several stretchers had been lined up in the back row; patients with advanced cases of leprosy lay with white cloths wrapped around their faces, listening to Ōsono's poem.

> 'Life in this world is a path of pain.
> No matter what trials I encounter,
> Until the very moment of death
> I will continue to tread that path.'

Egi of course had no idea who had composed the poem. And he did not know why Ōsono had deliberately selected such a disquieting verse for this occasion. Except for intermittent coughs from various corners of the room, the auditorium was hushed. As the long poem continued, several women with balding heads dabbed at their eyes with handkerchiefs or the corners of their blankets.

'Iijima . . .' Egi said abruptly. 'Why don't we do something for the group?'

'Us?' A mocking smile crossed his lips. Then, careful not to be seen by Satō and the other students who were watching the stage from the dressing-room, Iijima twisted the fingers of his hand into a gnarled claw. 'Even if we end up like this?'

Again Egi thought of the gash on his knee and the white membrane of skin that veiled it. He threw open the dressing-room door and hurried outside. A dark, oppressive silence hung over the deserted exercise ground and the fields blanketed with rain-clouds. Far in the distance he could hear the faint sound of a train passing through Gotemba. 'You're a despicable bastard,' he wanted to shout at himself. 'A wretched, disgusting, despicable bastard!'

The Christian students' programme finished some thirty minutes later. Egi looked on from a window facing the courtyard until every last one of the patients had left the assembly hall. First the women retired, then the male patients. Many of them limped or walked with canes. Finally the most seriously afflicted were carried out on stretchers by their more able comrades. Those not on stretchers were carried on the shoulders of their friends.

Satō led the students back to the reception room, where they were treated to milk and bread with jam, items that were hard to come by in Tokyo. Iijima, who stared at the wall of the room as he gnawed on his bread, suddenly asked the old administrator, 'Do they play baseball here?' A framed photograph on the wall, depicting several patients dressed in uniforms and carrying bats standing beside two or three nurses, had prompted his question.

'They certainly do. Of course, it's just the healthier ones.' Satō smiled his toothless smile. 'I don't know anything about baseball myself, but I understand they're very good at it.'

'Hey, Ōsono!' Iijima called to Ōsono, whose face was still flushed from the excitement of the performance. 'Why don't you guys have a game of baseball with the team here?'

This was clearly Iijima's spiteful way of mocking the Christian students. Anybody – Iijima's words implied – can be philanthropic if all you have to do is stand up on a stage and look down at the inmates and sing songs and recite poetry; but why don't you have a go at baseball, where you'll actually have to come into physical contact with them?

'Why shouldn't we play? How about it, everybody?' Ōsono took up the challenge. 'Mr Satō, can you lend us some gloves?'

'We do have some the staff members use.' Once again the old man did his best to smooth over a delicate situation. 'You know, you really don't have to do this.'

Ōsono stood up, and the rest of the Christian students followed him reluctantly. Some nurses, oblivious to what was going on, cheerfully brought in some mitts and gloves and then scurried over to the infirmary to tell the patients about the game.

When they reached the playing field, the students put on their borrowed gloves and grudgingly began tossing the ball back and forth. Somehow their throws lacked vitality. A chilly breeze blew in from the direction of the fields.

'Hey, Egi!' Ōsono turned unexpectedly and called out. 'Come and play with us.'

He flung an extra glove at Egi. Egi cast a quick, pained look in Iijima's direction, but his friend was standing with his back to the group, staring at the fields with his hands thrust into his overcoat pockets.

A cheer rang out from the infirmary. Patients of both sexes were pressing their faces against every window, waving their hands or white handkerchiefs. The hospital team had just come running out of the infirmary, dressed in mud-stained uniforms.

At first glance, the patients looked no different from normal, healthy people. But when they lined up in front of the students and politely removed their caps to bow and say 'Thank you', Egi noticed that some of them had bald patches the size of large coins on the tops of their heads, while the lips of others were cruelly twisted out of shape.

Standing in the outfield, Egi shut his eyes and tried to recall the scene he had witnessed in the assembly hall. The terminal patients, lying back with white cloths wrapped around their faces, listening to Ōsono's clumsy poetry recitation; their companions who carried them on their backs when it was all over. The women and young girls who sat with drooping heads, their hands resting neatly on their laps. And Egi himself, who had tried to turn his back on all of them. 'You rotten bastard. You worthless, contemptible wretch.' The words formed again inside his mouth. He struggled to exorcize the image of his wounded knee as it flickered before his eyes.

The game proceeded. The students' turn at fielding ended, and somehow they had managed to hold off the patients' attack and keep them scoreless. Their opponents were more formidable than they had expected.

'Egi, you're up to bat next,' someone called. From the corner of his eyes, Egi saw a thin, derisive smile appear on the lips of Iijima, who was watching the game just off to one side.

When Egi picked up his bat and started for the plate, Iijima walked up beside him, as though he were going to suggest a batting strategy.

'Hey, Egi,' Iijima whispered perversely, his breath smelling foul. 'You're afraid, aren't you? You're going to get infected!'

Egi resolutely swung his bat. It connected firmly, and the white ball went sailing into the distance. 'Run!' someone shouted. Frantically, Egi rounded first base and continued running, but the first baseman had already caught the ball from the third and had started after Egi. Caught between two bases, Egi suddenly realized that the hand that would touch him with the ball belonged to a leper. He stopped dead in his tracks. 'Keep going!' he told himself, and sprinted off again. The first baseman threw the ball to the second baseman. When he got a close-up view of the second baseman's receding hairline and gnarled lips, Egi's body was no longer willing to respond to the promptings of his conscience. He stopped, hoping to be able to dodge his opponent, and looked up nervously at the approaching patient.

In the patient's eyes Egi saw a plaintive flicker, like the look in the eyes of an abused animal.

'Go ahead. I won't touch you,' the patient said softly.

Egi felt like crying when he was finally by himself. He stared vacantly at the infirmary, which now looked somehow like a livestock shed, and at the silver fields beneath the overcast sky. And he thought, 'Thanks to my fear of physical pain, I'll probably go on betraying my own soul, betraying love, betraying others. I'm a good-for-nothing, a wretch . . . a base, cowardly, vile, despicable bastard.'

Drawing by Giorgio de Chirico, from his novel *Hebdomeros*

Cora Sandel

CORA SANDEL was born in Oslo in 1880, the daughter of upper-middle-class parents. Intending to become a painter, she moved to Paris at the age of twenty-five, where she lived in poverty on the fringes of the contemporary art scene for fifteen years. In 1913 she married a Swedish sculptor and lived with him in France and Sweden. They had one son. After their divorce in 1926, to support herself and her child she began to write. For many years she had a struggle to survive economically, at one point being reduced to pawning her typewriter. She was best known for her novels, particularly the *Alberta* trilogy, a powerful study of a woman's growth to self-knowledge and independence in Norway and Paris. Alberta herself is a profoundly modern protagonist, struggling to survive within the alienating conventions of her bourgeois environment. However, Sandel also wrote many shorter works which rank among her finest writings and created a hybrid dramatic and fictional form which she termed '*interior med figurer*' (interior with figures), one of which is the acclaimed *Krane's Café*, published in 1946. She has often been compared to Colette – whose work she translated into Norwegian – in her life, her feminist politics and in the experimental boldness of her work. She died in 1974.

'Nothing Cora Sandel writes could be a bore. She has a place to herself among the finest contemporary writing.' – *Guardian*

Alberta *and* The Silken Thread

Both these stories are taken from the collection *The Silken Thread*, first published by Peter Owen in 1986.

Alberta

GRANDMAMA IS ILL – dangerously ill. It says so in the telegram that is lying open and spread out on the living-room table.

Mama is going to travel to Grandmama. She ought to have gone long ago, when Grandmama was taken ill, but it's such an expensive journey.

When the telegram arrived Papa said that of course – of *course* – Mama must go, wherever the money was going to come from. Of course she must just do her packing and get ready.

But the worst of it is, Mama ought to have gone long ago, and now she may get there too late, even though the boat is leaving in a couple of hours.

She goes up to pack, sniffling. Her eyes are red and her lips pressed tightly together. Every now and then she expels a long, deep sigh.

Papa has disappeared into his study. The atmosphere is stormy.

Alberta dithers around the suitcase, attempting to make herself useful and, if possible, to dissipate the storm. She doesn't know what to do with her cold hands, and wrings them as if freezing. With all her strength she exerts herself to appear sympathetic towards Mama, but her conscience is guilty, because all the time she is thinking about Papa in his study.

'Isn't there anything I can help you with?' She tries cautiously, since the last thing that happened was that Mama irritably took something which Alberta had brought her straight out of her hands and put it back on the table.

'No, thank you, my dear Alberta,' she said in that cold, bitter voice which Alberta dreads more than anything. 'You're only getting in my way. Leave me alone.'

Now Alberta knows very well that it will be wrong if she does leave her alone. Her palms are beginning to sweat. She moves out of Mama's way and keeps as quiet as possible.

Suddenly Mama, kneeling in front of the suitcase with her face bent over it, exclaims, 'And your father doesn't think of giving me a single little thing for the journey, Alberta. Never the least thoughtfulness – never the slightest little attention. I can't tell you how much it hurts me, now when I need to feel a little love about me. I feel so lonely, so lonely.'

Mama's voice is choked with sobs, and Alberta watches the tears roll slowly down over her cheekbones and disappear into the suitcase.

Then Mama puts in Grandmama's photograph.

'Like this picture of your grandmother, Alberta. It's been standing on the bedside table for years, getting faded and ugly and ruined, but it has never occurred to your father to give me a little frame for it. Only a small thing, of course, but . . .'

Mama sniffs into the suitcase.

Alberta wrings her hands so that they risk being put out of joint. If her life were to depend on it, she would not know what to answer. When Mama calls Papa 'your father', it's like a warning bell.

Suddenly a door opens and someone calls 'Alberta!'

It's Papa.

When Alberta enters the study he is standing at his desk, holding a five-kroner piece in one hand. In the other is his open wallet. Alberta approaches him, her heart thumping.

'Look, Alberta,' says Papa, 'here's five kroner. Could you find some little thing for Mama that she might like to have on the journey? A small bottle of eau-de-Cologne, perhaps? I thought she might like it, and then I thought that now you're such a big girl, Alberta, you might go and buy it for Papa. I have so much to do, you know.'

Alberta catches her breath for relief and joy. *Could* she go and buy that little thing? Of course she could.

'Yes,' she says eagerly, 'of course I can. But I know of something that Mama wants much more than eau-de-Cologne, Papa.'

'What's that, Alberta?'

'She'd like a frame for Grandmama's picture,' exclaims Alberta, terrified lest she may not get it.

'Yes,' says Papa, 'but I'm sure she'd prefer some eau-de-Cologne for the journey. She can always have a frame some other time.'

'Oh no, Papa, no! I know she wants a frame. Nothing would please her more than a frame.'

'All right, all right,' says Papa. 'If you think so. Do as you think. That's the best thing, Alberta. I have so much work to do, as you see.'

Papa gestures at the desk and sits down. And he rubs his glasses before positioning them in front of his reddened eyes, which always look so tired.

Alberta reassures him yet again, 'Yes, Papa, yes', and hurries out.

After a while she returns from the hardware store on the corner with a piece of thick, polished glass which, with the help of a prop behind it, stands on two brass knobs. She has chosen it instead of all kinds of frames with metal scrolls and flourishes, and she feels certain she has chosen with good taste. She creeps on tiptoe through the kitchen and hall into Papa's study.

'Yes,' says Papa, looking at the object over his glasses, 'it's all right, but . . . I must say I think it would have been better to get some eau-de-Cologne,' he adds. 'But take it in to Mama, then. You go in and give it her, Alberta. You can say it's from you children.'

Alberta goes out quietly and hangs up her coat. Then she goes in to Mama through the dining-room.

Mama looks up from the suitcase. The barometer is quite unmistakably pointing to storm.

'Ah, there you are. May I ask where you've been? Not one of you thinks of giving me any help, not even you, Alberta. I thought I could count on a little help from my big daughter, but I see I was mistaken. You all leave me alone to . . .'

Mama's voice is lost in a sob.

'Mama,' says Alberta, feeling a choking sensation in her throat that makes it difficult to get the words out. 'Mama, I've been to buy this for you.'

'What is it?' says Mama, and her voice is so cold. Oh, Mama's cold voice. She takes the packet and unwraps the paper.

'Whatever is this? But, my dear Alberta . . . ?

'It's, it's . . .' stammers Alberta, her composure already lost. 'It was Papa who – but then I said that I thought. . . . It's from us children . . .'

She gets no further, for Mama interrupts her. 'What an extraordinary idea! If only he had bought a little eau-de-Cologne or something nice for the journey – the kind of thing other husbands think of when their wives travel.'

Mama's voice is like ice.

But inside Alberta something is jumping so oddly. Now she can feel that strange, painful pressure in her chest, as if her heart were turning over. And then will come the tears, that violent weeping that she cannot control. She knows it will. It's in her throat already, as she turns and runs out through the door.

Nothing irritates Mama more than Alberta's weeping.

And she rushes out and grabs the key to the only place where she can whimper and sob her heart out without embarrassing anyone.

The Silken Thread

THE AIR IN the studio is heavy and dry, as it usually is when you have had a model there for hours on end.

Rosina is telling me about the silkworm. She is sitting on the dais with her legs drawn up under her limbs, young and firm, but with something worn and slightly flabby about her body, as if she had been plump and had suddenly become thin. She is a warm golden colour, like a fruit matured by the sun. The narrow head with the tired face, aged too soon, is thrown back slightly; the brown eyes – usually veiled and turned inwards – are shining moistly. She draws her upper lip back over her white teeth in a broad smile, sweet and sad.

And suddenly one sees that Rosina must be telling the truth: that she is only twenty.

She hasn't told me much about herself. She hasn't the usual failings of a model: no upper-class family that she has broken with, no distinguished but strict father, who would kill her if he knew she was posing, and no mother who would die of shame. Nor is her father a childhood friend of President Poincaré, and she has not been educated in a convent among the daughters of the nobility.

And, the strangest thing of all: she hasn't taken me into her confidence about great artistic projects, about secret rehearsals, impending stage débuts or negotiations with impresarios at the Café de Globe.

All I know about Rosina is that she is from Asti and has spent three years in Paris and that she has the dogged tenacity of northern Italy in her work and the melancholy dreaminess of southern Italy in her eyes. Now she is lively and talkative all of a sudden on account of a silken thread that has attached itself to her. She twists the thread round her finger and stares at it. Then she holds it up in front of me and says, 'Silk's beautiful, isn't it?'

'Yes, it is, Rosina.'

'Strange to think that small animals make it.'

'Yes, Rosina. Have you ever seen silkworms?'

'Of course, signora! We had silkworms at home. We produced silk and sold it. Have you never seen how it's done, signora?'

'No. How is it done, Rosina?'

And so Rosina is set free on the path of candour, where we so easily gallop a little further than we would wish. It looks so innocent to begin with. One starts out so far from the great confidences. Even the most secretive of us are occasionally responsive to the little flick of the whip that chases us on. Rosina has been given it by the silken thread.

She tells me how the eggs are collected in the autumn and put under glass for the winter, and how in the spring they are carefully placed between pillows close to the warmth, how the whole house is warmed and how quickly and cautiously everyone moves about, so that no draughts will get in.

After a few days the pillows are teeming with tiny black larvae, each the size of a pinhead. If you offer them a mulberry leaf they will cling to it in their hundreds until it is completely covered, and in this way they are transferred to large wooden shelves made specially for the purpose. There they sit eating and growing, eating and growing for twenty days. They eat at an incredible rate. Bundles of leaves are carried in to them, and only the little pithy skeleton remains, stripped neat and tidy.

Day by day they grow while you watch. When twenty days have passed they are long and thick as a finger and can no longer be transported on mulberry leaves, because they are too heavy. When they have to be taken to the long dried stalks where they are to sir and spin themselves into their own silk, they must be picked up with the fingers – and it takes courage to pick up the fat little beasts with your fingers.

One day they stop eating. Then they are placed on blocks of wood. And then the spinning begins.

'It's interesting, signora, it's exciting, believe me. You can't think of anything else as long as it's going on. You watch them all the time and talk about which one will be good and which one will not turn out well. You don't talk about anything else.

'And then comes the big day when they are taken carefully off the stalks they're sitting on and sent in baskets to the silk factory. Then the whole family is busy – everyone helps. It's like a party, signora. But you have to touch them lightly, you have to pick them off gently, so that they're not torn to pieces.

'Silk cocoons are beautiful, signora, like a delicate, brittle little eggshell of mother-of-pearl.

'But it's a busy time, as you can imagine, it makes work. And then there are the hens who have their chickens at the same time, and the guinea pigs have their babies, and the rabbits.'

I sit wondering what can have driven Rosina away from all this, since it makes her voice warm and her face young to talk about it.

Then she says, 'And the bad cocoons were for me. I was allowed to sell them all on my own. I could earn eight to ten lire a time, if I kept my wits about me.'

'What did you do with the money, Rosina?'

The question slips out as so many questions do – any question, just for the sake of asking. What could a Rosina do with eight to ten lire a year?

'What did I do with it, signora? You'll never guess what I did with it.'

Rosina adopts a mysterious expression and puts a finger to her lips. She is no longer merely young, she is a child, mischievous and serious at the same time, as children can be. And she was beautiful as a child, maybe no more than three years ago.

'I hid the money, signora. I hid it under the roof thatch. I crept up when I was certain that no one was watching me, and I made a hollow in the thatch, to put the money in. One day there was more than fifty lire.

'I travelled with that money, signora.'

Rosina has become thoughtful. After a while she says, 'It's strange, Mother was so kind to me that day. It was almost as if she suspected something.'

'Wasn't your mother always kind to you, Rosina?'

'No. She was strict, signora, too strict. She scolded me all the time. That's why I knew for many years that I would leave when I could. And one day I went to the station and took the train, and since then I've heard nothing from home. I wrote once from here, in Paris, but nobody answered. They're cross with me at home.

'Parents are foolish to scold their children all the time, signora.'

'Yes, Rosina.'

'I came first to Chambéry. That's just across the border. I got a place there as a housemaid. I've worked all the time, signora, I've always been honest. And later on I went to Grenoble, where I was in service with the justice of the peace. Oh, I had a good place in Grenoble. Everyone smiled at me, and everyone was kind, and I didn't have much to do. Mostly I answered the door when anyone rang the bell, and I wore little white aprons and a little white cap on my head, and everyone thought I was sweet – oh yes, signora, I was so young then.

'But the daughters of the house were beautiful, you know, and so kind, especially the eldest. When she got married I stood there the whole time and received the guests, and many of them gave me a tip. Oh, everybody was kind on that occasion, signora. And in the evening, when the newly-weds left, we all cried. Her mother cried and her father cried, and her brother cried and her sister, and I did too. But the bride didn't cry.'

'Was there a brother too?'

'Yes, of course, and he was kind too, too kind, Signora. His mother didn't like it. Imagine, one evening he wanted to show me something in his room, and when we went through the salon we had to take our shoes off so that no one should hear us. And guess what, Madame turned up and saw us in our stockinged feet, both of us hand in hand. It was funny, signora. It was comical. But the next day I had to leave.'

'And then, Rosina?'

'Well, then I met my friend, my first friend . . .'

'Your first friend.'

'He had known me when I was with the justice of the peace, he had come to the house. He rented a room for me and bought me pretty clothes. But two weeks later he gave me money so I could travel to Paris. It didn't work out.'

'And then?'

'And then. Well, since then things have gone well,' says Rosina quickly, as if she thought it necessary to make that remark first. 'I've always had work. I've always been earning, except for the time I was in hospital. I've been a model all the time, signora, and I have my room and my own things. I'm alone when I'm there.

'I expect I'll go home one day, but not until I've saved a bit and can take a suitcase of pretty clothes with me. Then nobody will say anything, you see.'

'What was the matter with you when you were in hospital. Rosina?'

'Oh –' Rosina looks down – 'things went wrong, you understand, in the fourth month, and then I became ill . . .'

I make no comment and Rosina adds, 'What was I to do, signora? What would you expect? I couldn't bring a child into the world. What would I have done when I got fat and ugly and couldn't pose any more? What was I going to do afterwards? For I wouldn't have sent the child to an orphanage . . .'

Her voice is raised and her face is flushed, and she gestures against me and against everything I am not saying but that she assumes I intend to say. 'Oh no, signora, no, no, no!'

'Are you well now, Rosina?'

'Oh no, I'm often in pain, signora. Something says tak-tak-tak inside my stomach when I walk fast and when I go up stairs. I often have to stand still because it hurts. At the hospital they say I won't get better without an operation. Sooner or later I'll have to let them do it.'

'Perhaps it would be best to do it sooner, Rosina, and get it over and done with.'

'Then I shall lose my friend, signora, I'll be sure to lose him if

I'm lying ill in bed. We must not be ill, signora, the men don't like it. We have to pretend there's nothing the matter.'

There's no answer to that. It's true. It's risky for us to be ill, whether we are a prosperous bourgeois housewife or a little Rosina in an artists' quarter in Paris. Most of us know it, and we keep going as long as we can without giving up. It's our last half-penny, in a manner of speaking. With it we can still achieve a little of all that our weakness needs: security and a little happiness – and peace and repose in two strong arms.

Fashion plate by Erté, *Les Esclaves de Salome*, from his autobiography
Erté: Things I Remember

Isabelle Eberhardt

ISABELLE EBERHARDT was born in Geneva in 1877, the illegitimate daughter of a former Russian Orthodox priest (and friend of Bakunin) and a German-Russian mother. Aged twenty, she travelled with her mother to North Africa where she spent most of the rest of her short and unconventional life. When her mother died six months after they arrived, she stayed on, travelling and writing. A transgressor of boundaries, she converted to Islam and wandered the Sahara on horseback often disguised as an Arab man, experiencing numerous sexual adventures, experimenting with drugs, developing an interest in Sufic mysticism and sometimes working under cover for the French colonial government in Algeria. The last may have been the cause of the attempt on her life in 1901 which forced her to leave the country, though she later returned after marrying an Arab. Fluent in six languages including Russian, French and Arabic, she wrote a series of articles for publications in Paris and North Africa under a pseudonym. In 1904 she was drowned by a flash flood that trapped her inside her house. After her death further writings came to light, including an unfinished novel, stories and her journals. Among these, a number of her vignettes and stories, collected as *Prisoner of Dunes* and *The Oblivion Seekers* (the latter translated by Paul Bowles), have been published by Peter Owen.

'A hazy image of her as a soul-sick Amazon of the desert has been recycled as each new generation rediscovers radical desert chic. Yet her writings, and her sheer modernity, stand up to mainstream scrutiny . . . The vignettes are valuable sketches of the reality of desert life . . . and her perception of Islam as a future force on the world stage has proved prophetic.' – *Daily Telegraph*

Outside

This piece is taken from the collection of writings *The Oblivion Seekers*, which was translated by Paul Bowles and first published by Peter Owen in 1988.

LONG AND WHITE, the road twists like a snake toward the far-off blue places, toward the bright edges of the earth. It burns in the sunlight, a dusty stripe between the wheat's dull gold on one side, and the shimmering red hills and grey-green scrub on the other. In the distance, prosperous farms, ruined mud walls, a few huts. Everything seems asleep, stricken by the heat of day. A chanting comes up from the plain, a sound long as the unsheltered road, or as poverty without the hope of change tomorrow, or as weeping that goes unheard. The Kabyl farmers are singing as they work. The pale wheat, the brown barley, lie piled on the earth's flanks, and the earth herself lies back, exhausted by her labour pains.

But all the warm gold spread out in the sunlight causes no glimmer of interest in the uncertain eyes of the wayfarer. His locks are grey, as if covered by the same dull dust that cushions the impact of his bare feet on the earth. He is tall and emaciated, with a sharp profile that juts out from beneath his ragged turban. His grey beard is untended, his eyes cloudy, his lips cracked open by thirst. When he comes to a farm or a hut, he stops and pounds the earth with his long staff of wild olive wood. His raucous voice breaks the silence of the countryside as he asks for Allah's bread. And he is right, the sad-faced wanderer. The sacred bread he demands, without begging for it, is his by right, and the giving of it is only a feeble compensation, a recognizing of the injustice that is in the world.

The wayfarer has no home or family. He goes where he pleases, and his sombre gaze encompasses all the vast African landscape. And he leaves the milestones behind, one after the other, as he goes. When the heat is too great and he has had enough walking, he lies down under the big pistachio tree on the side hill, or at the foot of a weeping eucalyptus beside the road. There in the shade he drops into a dreamless sleep.

It may be that at one time it was painful for him to be homeless, to possess nothing, and doubtless also to have to ask for that which his instinct told him was due him in any case. But now, after so many years, each like the last, he has no more desires. He merely undergoes life, indifferent to it.

Often the gendarmes have arrested him and thrown him into prison. But he has never been able to understand, nor has anyone explained to him, how a man can be prohibited from walking in the life-giving light of day, or why those very men who had failed to give him bread or shelter should then tell him that it was *forbidden* not to possess these things.

When they accused him of being a vagabond, always he said the same thing: I haven't stolen. I've done nothing wrong. But they claimed that was not enough, and they would not listen to him. This struck him as unjust, like the signposts along the highways that illiterates had to understand.

The tall, straight back grew bent, and his gait became uncertain. Old age arrived early to exact its payments for his shattered health. He suffered from the wretched illnesses of old age, those ailments whose very cure brings no consolation to the patient, and one day he fell beside the road. Some pious Moslems found him there and carried him to a hospital. He said nothing.

But there the old man of the wide horizons could not bear the white walls, the lack of space. And that spongy bed did not feel as good as the ground that he was used to. He grew depressed and longed for the open road. If he stayed there, he felt, he would merely die, without even the solace of familiar sights around him.

They handed him back his ragged clothes with disgust. He was not able to go very far, and he collapsed before he got out of the city. A policeman came up to him and offered to help him. The old man cried: 'If you're a Moslem, leave me alone. I want to die outside. Outside! Leave me alone.'

The policeman, with the respect of those of his religion for the penniless and the deranged, went away. The wayfarer dragged himself beyond the hostile city and fell asleep on the soft ground beside a faintly trickling stream. Covered by the friendly dark, and with the vast emptiness around him, he fell into an untroubled sleep. Later, he felt stronger, and he began to walk straight ahead, across the fields and through the scrub.

The night was drawing to an end. A pale glow came up behind the black line of the mountains in Kabylia, and from the farms the cocks' cracked voices called for daylight. He had slept on an embankment which the first rains of autumn had covered with grass. The cyclamen-scented breeze brought with it a penetrating chill. He was weak; a great weariness weighted his arms and legs, but the cough that had come with the arrival of the cold air now bothered him less.

It was daylight. From behind the mountains shone a red dawn, making bloody streaks on the calm surface of the sea, and dyeing the water with golden splotches. The faint mist that still hung above the ravines of Mustapha disappeared, and the countryside came nearer, huge, soft, serene. No broken lines, no clash of colour. One would have said that the earth, lying back in exhaustion, still permitted itself a sad and slightly sensual smile. And the wayfarer's arms and legs grew heavier.

He thought of nothing. No desires, no regrets. Softly, in the solitude of the open spaces, the uncomplicated and yet mysterious force that had animated him for so many years, fell asleep inside him. No prayers, no medicines, merely the ineffable happiness of dying.

The first tepid rays of sunlight, filtering through damp veils of eucalyptus leaves, gilded the motionless profile, the closed eyes, the hanging rags, the dusty bare feet and the long olivewood staff: everything that the wayfarer had been. The soul no one suspected him of possessing had been exhaled, a murmur of resignation from ancient Islam, in simple harmony with the melancholy of life.

Yoko by John Lennon, from *Grapefruit* by Yoko Ono

Octavio Paz

OCTAVIO PAZ was born in Mexico in 1914. He was one of the finest poets to write in Spanish in the twentieth century and one of the most significant Latin American literary figures of the period, as well as a philosopher, essayist and critic. His mother was of pure Spanish descent, but his father had Mexican Indian blood, a fact of which Paz was very proud, and the celebration of Mexico's pre-Columbian heritage informed his work. He was politically active on the left, but, as in all things, he was a maverick who found it hard to toe any party line and grew very hostile towards Stalinism. While in the diplomatic corps in Paris in the 1940s he became associated with André Breton and the surviving Surrealist circle. Between 1962 and 1968 he was Mexican ambassador to India, but he resigned in protest at the brutal suppression of student demonstrations in Mexico City. He was awarded the Nobel Prize for Literature in 1990 and died in Mexico City in 1998.

'The Word – or lack of it – is at the heart of the prose and poetry of the Mexican genius Octavio Paz. "In order to be able to speak, learn to be silent," was one of his best-known aphorisms. Paz was a man of words and a man of silences.' – James Kirkup, *Independent*

A Poet

This piece is taken from the collection of prose poems *Eagle or Sun*, first published by Peter Owen in 1990.

'MUSIC AND BREAD, milk and wine, love and sleep: free. Great mortal embrace of enemies that love each other: every wound is a fountain. Friends sharpen their weapons well, ready for the final dialogue to the end of time. The lovers cross the night enlaced, conjunction of stars and bodies. Man is the food of man. Knowledge is no different from dreaming, dreaming from doing. Poetry has set fire to all poems. Words are finished, images are finished. The distance between the name and the thing is abolished; to name is to create, and to imagine, to be born.'

'*For now, grab your hoe, theorize, be punctual. Pay your price and collect your salary. In your free time, graze until you burst: there are huge meadows of newspapers. Or, blow up every night at the café table, your tongue swollen with politics. Shut up or make noise: it's all the same. Somewhere they've already sentenced you. There is no way out that does not lead to dishonour or the gallows: your dreams are too clear*, you need a strong philosophy.'

Illustration by Roland Topor, from *Topor: Stories and Drawings*

Jeremy Reed

JEREMY REED was born in Jersey, Channel Islands. Novelist, biographer, essayist, critic and poet, he has been a prize-winner of the National Poetry Competition and has won a major Eric Gregory Award. His poetry collection *By the Fisheries* earned him the Somerset Maugham Award in 1985. Peter Owen has published seven of Reed's novels – including *Dorian, When the Whip Comes Down* and *Chasing Black Rainbows*, from which the following extract is taken – and six works of non-fiction.

'The imagination of this remarkable writer illuminates a unique landscape.' – J.G. Ballard

Chasing Black Rainbows

The following extract is from *Chasing Black Rainbows*, a novel based on the life of the French dramatist, poet, actor and theoretician of the Surrealist movement, Antonin Artaud (1896–1948). The historical Artaud was diagnosed as a schizophrenic, but in Reed's novel he is recast as an anarchic visionary who subverts bourgeois values through the power of his imagination. The fictional Artaud, his lover Anaïs Nin, her lovers Henry and June Miller, Artaud's psychiatrist Dr Ferdière and his patient Denise become intertwined in a tale of subtly delineated eroticism.

I HAD HEARD of Artaud through Anaïs. I had been made familiar with his ravings, hallucinations, the tortured complexity of his emotions. But here I was, confronting a different person. He was desperately poor like all those who live from poetry. His hands shook. Thunder skies travelled across the surface of his eyes. They shifted from clear to storm with an irregularity which was fascinating. He was serious to the exclusion of humour as well as trivia. He made it clear that the involuntary commitment to life, and the greater responsibility of preparing for one's death, were his singular preoccupation. Creativity was the expression he believed should be given to living. And he treated me as his immediate accomplice. He wanted a whisky. A second one. And a third. I was glad to keep pace with his intake. He was fired by the liquor. He grew distraught in describing his creative struggle. I remember his words: 'I am vegetating. I can neither advance nor retreat. I am fixed, localized around a point which is always the same. To go beyond that, I need to live. And I refuse to live. The point is that my thought no longer develops either in space or in time. And what comes out of me does so as if by chance. I have the notion it's independent of who I am. And if I expressed myself in terms that meant the opposite, would it matter? I need heroin to escape this trap.'

As he spoke, he was looking around for a dealer. I could see that he was used to buying street drugs, that he took the risk of being apprehended in possession. There was a young man who kept returning to the street. He stood with his back to the wall and waited. He could sense Artaud's need. He had become the centre of Artaud's world. He had the substance to placate craving. He was visibly poor and on drugs. His eyes found nothing but Artaud's own ravaged body, as though he had eliminated the rest of the species. And I couldn't leave him suffer. I got out a bundle of notes from my pocket-book, and placed them in his hand.

He was gone immediately. The young man slipped inside a bar, as though totally disinterested in Artaud's approach. The deal must have taken place inside, for Artaud returned with a sachet of white powder. 'It's a means of slowing the tornado,' he said. It was his private ritual, something that distinguished him from the crowds. And he must have recognized in me someone sympathetic. Could he tell that I too had experimented with altered states of consciousness? He was calmer after he had secured his supply. Heroin was one thing, and opium another. 'What I like about opium,' he confided, 'is that the body of soft flesh and white wood given me by I don't know what father-mother is, under its use, transformed. I become someone else. I live in reality.' His eyes expressed the suffering that drove him in search of drugs, and a defiance to stand by that decision. I kept thinking that this extraordinary meeting really was intended. We were outsiders sharing our thoughts, protecting them from a hostile capital.

He spoke with passionate conviction. The mad were those who dared speak the truth. They were attuned to a different form of reality. He was warm about Breton, and the Surrealist pursuit of the marvellous, and aggressive about his expulsion from the group on political grounds. 'Poetry,' he told me, 'is a conflagration. Its language is the vocabulary of authentic vision.' He wanted another whisky. I imagined he would use the heroin later. He was burning up on nerve. His voice would rise from a whisper to a declamatory shriek. People would stare, but the protective circle we had formed round each other was inviolable. I wasn't in the least frightened by his unpredictable shifts of mood. I was his friend without knowing him. We were acting out our moment of time on earth. It was our business and nobody else's.

I can still remember fragments of his heated monologue, lyrical gestures that accompanied his gentle moments. And the latter came as pauses in between his more urgently consuming preoccupations. He was a man set on a dynamic preparation for death. The other things, the little things of life, didn't matter to him. 'I am miserable like a man who has lost the best of himself,' he told me. 'What I seek to isolate and surround, what I want to know at least once in my life, is that point of thought where, having cast off the commonest illusions and temptations of language, I find myself confronting a state of mind which is absolutely naked, absolutely clear and without ambiguity or confusion. The blinding experience which rips through all the layers of reality.'

He banged his fist on the table. The waiter brought two more whiskies. We were getting high in Pigalle, the clouds tumbling on a slipstream into the future. When I looked up, the sky was too blue. I thought I could see through its transparency to a couple sitting at a table up above the clouds. They were screened by a red umbrella. The sun was setting on their lives.

Anaïs, Henry, my other friends and problems were left behind. The universe existed in this man. He could have led me into the fire and I would have gone his way, my skirt caught by red and yellow flames. Artaud's intensity hummed like the space inside a clenched fist. If I'd placed my head against his, I would have heard the Atlantic Ocean breaking across an autumn beach. If I'd looked too deeply into his eyes, I would have seen horses being castrated, statues shifting position, the sea in collision with the sky. I would have seen a man attempting to defy temporal limitations. Someone whose poetry burnt into the abdomen. His voice was nearer now. 'This is why I wish to describe the full extent and the full desolation of my pain which is, I believe, without precedent and without any kind of comparison possible.

I am called mad because my vision subverts governments. If you listen to me, you will be initiated into truth.'

I didn't care that my short black skirt had ridden up to the level of my stocking-tops. The obscene comments of passers-by were irrelevant to the universal discoveries we were sharing. What men observed on a crotch level was very different from the vertical axis on which I was floating. Artaud's being was a dynamic of constrained ballistics. 'And what is an authentic madman? It's a man who has preferred to go mad, in the sense in which society understands the term, rather than be false to a certain idea of accepted human behaviour. That is why society has had all those of whom it wanted to rid itself, and against whom it wanted to defend itself, because they had refused to become its material accomplices, condemned to be brutalized in asylums. For a madman is also a man to whom society refused to listen, and whom it wanted to prevent from divulging unbearable truths.'

I listened to the authenticity of a man speak from an unmodified inner voice. He had no need to edit or moderate his thought. And this was his trouble. He wouldn't compromise. He despised the corrupt, those who sacrificed the pursuit of their inner lives to business. He believed that truth was answerable only by the systematic elimination of all political intrusion on the individual's inner freedom. He attacked language that was used to validate an ideological lie. He wanted to go back to the more primitive roots of shamanism in which the body is the gestural organism for received inspiration.

He hoped to rebuild his theatre. His Alfred Jarry Theatre and his Theatre of Cruelty had both failed ignominiously. Lack of proper finance, and the extremism of Artaud's beliefs in theatre had brought him into confrontation with the public. He wanted to set fire to the stage, drive the placid bourgeoisie out into the street with their hair in flames. For Artaud, as for Sade before him, theatre was an expression of madness. It represented anarchy raised to the eloquence of poetic speech. 'I give up my fear in the sound of rage, in a directed roaring.'

A cold wind was frisking the street, turning over the dusty plane leaves. He didn't appear to notice; he would have commented on it had the wind been inside his head. And without ordering them, there were suddenly more drinks. It was as though all subliminal wishes materialized in his presence.

Each time I crossed my legs, I felt the sensual friction of silk come alive on my skin. But it wasn't physical desire I felt for this man, it was fascination at his difference. This was the person who had told Anaïs that it would thrill him to crucify her. He had claimed that, between them, there could be a murder. But I didn't sniff potential violence in him toward individuals. If he had been strait-jacketed at times, it was due to his rage at a system of things that allowed so little room for individual expression.

What Artaud wanted was a poetry that incorporated danger and concerted action into its field. He chewed on his cigarette. He bit it in the urgency of his speech, and when it snapped free, he crushed it like an offending insect. He was visibly at odds with his body clock. He resented the passing of time, for he would like to have strangled the moment, wrung its neck, and extracted from it the meaning of his pain.

A sailor lurched towards our table and wouldn't go away. He was unpeeling a wad of notes from his pocket. He wanted me at any cost. The bulge in his pants was like a papaya fruit. I wouldn't allow him to break into the hypnotic train of our speech. He *was* stroking himself in his torment, his eyes fixed on my black-stockinged legs. 'What's the price of some fun, darling? Take me upstairs and I won't ship out in the morning.' He kept on and on with his urgent solicitations. He was clearly English and half drunk. 'Whadya dressed like that for, if you're not a tart?' His demands were growing to a form of salacious incantation, and the waiters did nothing. Perhaps they were taking revenge on me for having seen me day after day casually patrolling these streets, indifferent to all advances. Or perhaps they were frightened of the sailor's confrontational stance.

Artaud appeared not to have heard or noticed the man. He

was entirely focused on the inner stream of thought to which he was giving expression. He was telling me of his struggle against the fixed academic conception of theatre, and how lack of spontaneous fluidity both in the writing and the acting of plays had given the public the notion theatre was dead. It was, he declared, 'a neuter activity, a subject for cafe gossip. Theatre is a donkey which has swallowed its own cock.' He was aggressive, spitting with vehemence. I imagined if he stood up the sailor would make a quick exit, but then he was gentle again, talking about the mauves, greens and oranges that distinguished a particular mood in the late afternoon sky, and comparing it to how women dressed on the boulevards. 'Like flowers, in perpetual sexual motion.' I loved him for that. This man, who spent so much time in the dark crystal at his interior, could still notice the beauty of women crossing Paris.

The sailor wouldn't back off. And having pushed the issue this far, in living out a fiction, I wasn't going to retreat. I could have placed my coat over my legs, but that would have been a concession to macho posturing. The part I knew I was acting was being taken literally by this wolfishly hungry sailor. His erection was telescoping to pop his buttons. This was worse than anything Henry would have staged in public. And if Artaud was conscious of what was happening, he chose to ignore it, or considered it gratuitous to his train of thought. He was talking about the necessity to devaluate written poetry, and the need to emphasize the spontaneous text. 'Written poetry is valuable once, and after that it should be destroyed. It's a question of knowing what we want. Let the dead poets make way for the new. Respect petrifies us.' I could feel the silent anger within him. I wanted him to keep on speaking, so that his words would exclude the sailor. I hung on to his speech as though it was a rope supporting me from a vertiginous drop. People at the bar were looking out half amused at the sailor's obstinate sexual demands. And when people are amused or curious, they remain detached spectators. No one was going to come to my assistance. They must have been secretly hoping that I would get up from the table and lead the sailor off to my apartment. They would have attached their eyes to my bottom, all the way down the street, imagining how my legs would go back over my head at the sailor's demands. They couldn't know that my intentions were radically to the contrary. That I wanted to dematerialize, find myself back in my apartment, safe in the complicitous dark of my bedroom.

I wasn't expecting the violent scene which ensued. Rather like a snake closing on another in diminishing circles, Artaud had waited. With electrified impulses, he got up from his chair, smashed his whisky glass on the pavement, and seethed at the sailor for his disrespect of the conversation. His rage was directed at the man's interfering with the spontaneity of his thought. 'Do you know who you are interrupting? Antonin Nalpas. The chosen one.'

The sailor was too shocked to respond, and too drunk to offer an offensive. He rocked back on his heels, hands reaching out for support holds. Artaud's explosive temper had blown the man out. I fumbled in my bag for money to take care of the drinks, and we left, Artaud immediately taking up his stream of consciousness without reference to the incident.

Illustration by Jean Cocteau, from *Le Livre Blanc*

Peter Vansittart

PETER VANSITTART was born in 1920 and educated at Haileybury and Worcester College, Oxford. He has taught and lectured on English and history, and he reviews for a number of national newspapers and periodicals. He is the author of more than forty works of fiction and non-fiction. Since 1968 Peter Owen has published fourteen of Peter Vansittart's critically acclaimed novels – including *Pastimes of a Red Summer*, *Parsifal* and *A Choice of Murder* – a work of non-fiction – *Worlds and Underworlds: Anglo-European History Through the Centuries* – and his memoirs, *Survival Tactics: A Literary Life*.

'Peter Vansittart is a wonderful novelist and storyteller.' – A.S. Byatt

Hermes in Paris

This extract comes from the middle of Peter Vansittart's most recent novel. Hermes – god, trickster and mischief-maker – is the protector of shepherds, travellers' guide, conductor of souls to the underworld, messenger of Zeus, bringer of good luck and patron of orators, writers, athletes, merchants and thieves. He visits Earth now and then looking for opportunities to play practical jokes and stir things up. He chooses to holiday in Paris at the time of the brilliant but unstable court of Napoleon III – another opportunist, conspiratorial and outwardly amiable – and the beautiful, nervy Empress Eugénie. Hermes finds much to provoke his laughter – and such laughter is dangerous. Under his influence France enjoys a succession of illusions involving the highest in the land, the comfortable middle classes and the journalists, poets and intellectuals of Left Bank cafés, and everything flows inexorably towards the most explosive joke that Hermes can devise.

WITHOUT WARNING, AS if by magician's cliché, in braggadocio display, fireworks were exploding above the palace, more millions, the tinted chips and flares spreading into the clusters of Bonaparte bees and violets that flew, halted, trembled, then shook themselves into an enormous N played upon by a novel electric searchlight, and suspended for an instant over Paris, France, the world. It dissolved, then, spirited from a constellation, emerald, scarlet, sapphire, blue as Eugénie's eyes, there blared the Imperial hymn, 'Partant Pour la Syrie', treacly but not wholly forgettable.

Groans and plaudits resumed for the roll-call of the Empire, flocking into the immense, illuminated structure: Bassanos, Esslings, Montebellos, Murats, Cambacerères, a Ney, Prince de la Moskowa, puppets of history, under the eye of Hermes. Also, Duchess de Morny, widow of Auguste, he of the *coup*, of Mexico, of Longchamp races. With her ambled Princess Walewski, relict of the late Foreign Minister, sired by Hercules himself on his Polish countess. The Princess was alleged to have allowed her favours to the Emperor, a tribute to His Majesty's taste.

Cheerful greetings were thrown at Countess de la Pöeze, so thin that Rochefort called her a needle seen sideways. Then a Mouchy, a Talleyrand, M. Viollet-le-Duc, so busy weighting France down with restored cathedrals, Dr Conneau, the Emperor's lifelong physician, fellow-prisoner at Ham. There the powerful Gallifet, there Marshal MacMahon. M. Dumas had been seen, without camellias, M. Gounod was said to have arrived, along with Count Benedetti, the Corsican, darkly self-assured French ambassador to Prussia.

Jeers proclaimed the arrival of Plon-Plon, the Emperor's cousin, Prince Napoleon, coarsened replica of Hercules; an intelligent radical, he had risked his intelligence in the Crimea where he was reputed to have shown cowardice, so that shouts of 'Craint Bomb' now made him glare and mutter. More Imperial relatives were inextricably mixed with Bourse magnates, lords of transport, hotel princelings, directors of agricultural colleges and electrical combines. One saw magnificos from the Bureau Arabe, the State Library, the Comédie Française, perhaps MM. Gautier, Sainte-Beuve, Delibes and a few of the artistic *gratin*, for the Emperor had founded a Salon des Refusés, thereby demonstrating contempt for conservatism, insensitivity to painting, compassion for losers or flair for the unexpected.

History was on the prowl, for there, between the flambeaux, kissing a polished, sparkling hand, was old Flahaut, another bastard, Talleyrand's, and perhaps . . . but no. He was swiftly enveloped by a cohort of stars, crosses, sashes, of heroes of the Crimea, Italy, Algeria – Pélissier, Leboeuf, Boubaki, Canrobert, pacing to the roll of unheard drums, the tread of grandeur, and statesmen, Ollivier, the Honourable Man, creator of the era of serenity and ideas, Rouher, once christened by Rochefort as 'the Man who said that All's Well in Mexico'. All were applauded for their glitter and dignity, though the din subsided into hostile silence for Baron Haussmann, with whom the Emperor had designed the New Paris and who received the blame for prodigal acquisitions and dislocations. Behind him, pleased with himself, was Antoine Agenor, Corsican careerist, now Duke de Gramont, singled out by Hermes, pleasantly amused, for particular attention. Tonight, however, he was barely noticed, for beneath further eruptions of fireworks another spectacular N, again hailed by artificial light, cheers were resounding for the hero of East and West, Ferdinand de Lesseps, whose Suez Canal, the Empire's feat of the century, had slapped the complacent face of England. Hermes' light cane might have saluted him, and also Monseigneur Bauer, tall, smooth, dapper in violet soutane of fashionable cut, murmuring 'Good Evening, Good Evening' as if bestowing absolution, a specimen whom a Hermes delights to collect. Formerly a Magyar atheist, political conspirator, photographer, artist, salesman, he was at present, thanks to the gay-go-up of the times, Imperial Almoner, Apostle Proto-notary, Confessor to Her Majesty. Hats were doffed, some knees were bent, until another silence announced the arrival of the Prussian Minister, heading other foreign notables: Metternichs, Grazianos, Schwarzenbergs, Kraczynskis, Mercy-Argenteaus.

Fanfare made visible, the bright gold N hovered on the night, a talisman, enduring amid the rainfalls of sparks, while a band played lively melodies from Auber, Gounod, Hérold, Meyerbeer, Waldteufel and from Offenbach's *Orfée*, which brought gods down even lower than Earth. Some singing seemed to rhyme with the delicate filigree above, formations of dazzling, ethereal bouquets, waves, cornucopias, white, scarlets, greens, purples, in arcs and circles and soaring, exploding ascents in constant rebirth.

Within, hours were suspended, moments were vast, tremulous as raindrops, a whisper, a wink, momentous as a treaty. The great windows, trimmed with gold leaf, curtains drawn aside, gleamed with the radiances without. Woven with intricate simplicities, though, Hermes must notice that, inexpertly hung, the Gobelins and Syrian hangings, in doubtful juxtaposition, yet gave medieval or paradisaical vistas, above which, through scents and cigar fumes, glimmered the naked allurements of Boucher ceilings. One passage reflected Meissonier's battlefields, heroic, tragic, another, the smiling ladies of Vigée Lebrun; an ante-room, where brilliance drooped, a doubtful Rubens, a presumed Andrea del Sarto were almost submerged in foliaged, will-o'-the-wisp half-lights which dulled the jewels and decorations, made eyes and mouths cruel or cunning, before moving back into the electric glare, through dense globes of hothouse lilies, roses, camellias.

Space was labyrinthine, always tempting one deeper, weighted by heavy, upholstered sofas, solid curtains, massive statuary, making ramparts against the streets. Lustrous mirrors were rimmed with a fantasia of cherubs, leaves, grapes, flutes, echoed by the fleeting expressions, exquisitely designed hairstyles, almost-naked breasts, of humans edging towards infinity.

Light-blue and white Cent-Gardes, the Emperor's Chosen, lined the curved, balustraded Grand Staircase, their heads flashing silver like cruets tufted and upturned. Scarcely mortal, motionless, they stared ahead at the measured ascent of world notables, each name a carillon. There was no uniform style, only jumbled, broken patterns. Skirts were hobbled, bustled, hooped, multi-panelled, very full, like bell-jars, or looped in a fashion once set by the Empress and much derided by the old aristocracy for degrading ladies to ballet-dancers. Long moiré gowns flaunted against short gowns of emeraldine satin, ivory-white satin, crêpes of frothy lace, Alençon and Valenciennes, geranium-pink velvet bobbed with crocus yellow, tulle trimmed with pale moons, cornflowers, fish-scales, shawls of lilac silk glistening within confections of tiaras, pendants, bracelets, brooches, puffed sleeves and bare arms, black frock-coats, golden coats, resplendent knee-breeches, trousers creamy, trousers striped blue and grey, flamboyant cravats of Americans and Jews, while, like leaves rustling, were the fans newly created by Duvelleray spreading tiny pictures of Japanese gardens, lakes and groves and scrambled with the wisdom of the Bonaparte Hercules. *Courage is like Love, it feeds on Hope.*

Ladies, and numerous gentlemen, were sprayed with jewels from Vechte, Payen Dotin, Froment-Meurice, the very latest, as if to exhibit would-be purity, like chastity adrift in a brothel. Beards and moustaches changed shapes yearly, imitating the ruler; dresses swelled, dwindled, deferring to Mr Worth, the Empress's favourite couturier. Red and gold automatons, the Court Chamberlains, incessantly bowed, to the fluffy and tulled, the frogged and epauletted, the over-courteous and the manifestly drunk. Robed, impassive Arabs tall in white and crimson, bouncy Italians, stern, soberly tailed and shirt-fronted English, Hungarian generals sashed and cross-sashed, Austrian noblemen in rainbow uniforms, Russian diplomats, South American hidalgos. A few rich, light auburn wigs, to honour the Empress. Opalescent chandeliers gently swayed with the murmurations beneath, their crystalline brilliants reflecting the multitudinous colours of Northern Lights or the gala fireworks.

Hermes would be at home here, as patron of secret dossiers, deceiving gestures, usurers masquerading as princes, smiling bankers and trusting borrowers disguised as *penseurs*. All could venture far, without very much movement, approaching Salle d'Apollon, Salle du Trône, Salle du Premier Consul, Salle Louis Quinze, Salle Blanche, Galérie de Diane, each with its particular colour, evanescent and, another compliment to the Empress, foggy with Peau d'Espagne. Mistaking a footman for a guest, a Portuguese gentleman confided that he felt as if encased in a Neapolitan ice-cream.

Illustration by Jean Cocteau, from his novel *The Miscreant*

Angela Green

Angela Green was born in 1949. She grew up in Kent, Scotland and Hampshire and read French at Kings College London. In the late 1990s she gave up a successful business career in order to write full time. She lives in Surrey with her husband and their two children and spends part of the year in southern Brittany. *Cassandra's Disk* is her first novel.

Cassandra's Disk

This is the opening chapter of *Cassandra's Disk*, a new novel following the fates of a pair of twin girls. Photographer Cassandra Byrd – giantess, eccentric and sexual siren – races against time to commit a raucous account of her highly unprincipled past to her computer. Realizing that her twin sister Helen has been born with a double share of beauty, talent and maternal love, Cassandra reinvents herself on her own terms as the vulgar, uninhibited 'Big Bad Baby'. Helen survives their catastrophic childhood to become a successful actress, and Cassandra sets out on a rampaging odyssey, secretly following her sister's sexual trail in order to prove her own attractiveness. She creates the strange photographic portrait that will make her name, *The Byrds*, featuring the two sisters naked and bird-masked, and for a while it seems that they will overcome their differences; but the relationship founders. During an attempt at a reconciliation in Greece Cassandra falls for Helen's new husband and, against his better instincts, he is drawn towards his wife's predatory twin, who uses all her skills to ensnare him, with tragic consequences.

Aghios Georghios, Ithaca
21 September 1999, 11.00 a.m.

They are coming down the corridor with tea. Earl Grey. A cup of smoky bergamot every two hours. Dr Mike approves of this surviving pleasure and so do I. Perfumed steam wafts warm against my forehead. When it is drained to the leaves, I settle the laptop back upon the starched linen and watch the cursor blink. My fingers are ringless, knuckled and brown; oddly, where they rest on the keyboard, they spell the word that describes their new appearance: T-H-I-N.

Begin.

Yes, but where? And how?

After years of looking at the world through a viewfinder, at first I see pictures – an album. It opens on a large baby, glowering in sepia arms.

Beyond are the deckle-edged black-and-white snapshots of childhood, then teenage years in sunbleached pastel. At the end, digital images sparkle like frost . . .

But no. Pictures are not enough. Memory is too trackless and vast to fit through the eye of a single lens; it cries out for a wider horizon – the infinite longitude and latitude of words.

My fingers stir on the keyboard, ready to cast the first tentative line down into the past . . .

I remember

Deeper . . .

I remember

Deeper . . .

I remember

Yes.

I remember a thunderstorm rolled over Hampstead on the night we were born, like a rattle from an announcing drum.

Ha! You see . . . the first lie!

Hey. Though at thirty-nine my memories are still as richly coloured and detailed as a book of hours, I cannot claim to have my namesake's clairvoyance. (Even though I *was* born with an ability to scale the walls of other minds and peer in at their thoughts – which has proved itself useful on occasion.) But to go back to the moment of my birth? Tricky, even for me.

'Do you think talking to someone would help?' asks Sister Andrew kindly. 'Perhaps not a priest, though Father Gregorio on Cephallonia is an excellent listener.'

Oh, please.

There are other ways round the problem. My way is this: instead of limiting myself to what can be remembered, whenever my memory blurs I shall gently turn the focus of my imagination. Unknown events and conversations will sharpen into obedient clarity and I shall look back with prescience to the past.

See?

In other words, I give fair warning: I shall lie a little.

Sometimes a lot.

So.
Begin again.
Where was I?

Where am I?

Birth

It is thirty-nine years ago and high over London I plane with lazy hawks on a dark May morning and watch the gathering of clouds.

Listen. Is that the thunder? Look down on the mosaic of streets and find the hospital. It was still there last time I was in Hampstead. Clarify now. There it is. See?

At 6 a.m. the sky behind the heath darkens to damson and Denise Byrd screams as lightning crackles down into the hospital gardens. Outside the labour ward window the burnt air smells of danger. My mother runs her hands back through her dripping blonde hair and screams again as the contractions come, heavy as a blind hydraulic press.

'Here's the first babe,' says Senior Midwife (her name is lost in time – what shall we call her? Atkins, I think, a reassuring, homely name and therefore one my mother would instinctively have disliked). 'Right. Push now. Push now, Mrs Byrd, love, come on.' The midwife glances at her watch; another hour and she'll be home at her flat in Swiss Cottage, sweeping the rainwater off the balcony and feeding the cats. 'Come on, my dear, make an effort now, we're nearly there.' These stuck-up women are the worst, in her experience, with all their indignant whimpering. Sister Atkins glances over at the pair of conferring doctors and taps my mother on her stirruped foot.

'Come on, dear, bear down, do.'

Clenching her teeth Denise strains forward. A broad, dark head advances steadily, pushing and stretching.

It is me.

Denise feels her tenderest flesh tear strand by strand. She grabs the metal handrail and outscreams the thunder, willing, *ordering* me to stop, but I drive on downwards, as I must do, stretching her further and further still. *Make way there.* We all hold our breath. Airless minutes, years, aeons pass, and at their end a wet red mass slithers out of my mother's body and lies between her legs.

I am here.

The midwife scoops me up and shows my mother her first-born.

'A girl, Mrs Byrd, a fine big girl. Look.'

My mother looks at my blood-smeared black hair, my greasy torso, the hanging, purplish cord that disappears inside her. She shudders in distaste and turns her head away. Mrs Atkins, who has seen it all before, cuts our cord and passes me to the young assistant nurse, who carries me to the far side of the delivery room to begin the ritual acknowledgement of my arrival: I am weighed (nearly nine pounds, not bad for a twin) and measured (twenty-three inches, well done!) and the worst of my mess is wiped from me.

Lying on the narrow bed, my mother suddenly feels her pelvis fill again and arches her tired body up in protest. But this time she need not worry. The rapidly emerging head is fair and small; a slender baby girl comes smoothly through the passage I have hewn for her. Denise breathes gratefully, and round blue eyes blink up into her face.

'Chalk and cheese, these two,' says Mrs Atkins brightly. 'Cheer up, my dear. Just look at this pretty little miss.'

I cannot see my sister, but I know she's here.

Years later, I find that we are not only twins but twins to the power of three, astrologically speaking. Every sign we have is in the house of Gemini.

RENOVABITVR

THE END

Illustration by Salvador Dalí, from his novel *Hidden Faces*

How Others See Us

'Hats off to Peter Owen for the remarkable books he has published for so many years. From Chirico and Dalí to Jeremy Reed and Anna Kavan, he has brought us the best of American and European writing. Never has an investment of £900 produced such vast riches.' – J.G. Ballard

'Peter Owen is the only firm I know that publishes, as well as good books by native authors, many worthwhile works from other languages which this country would be intellectually poorer and more isolated without. He deserves the gratitude of all those many readers who want to know what literature is being produced in other countries. Many thanks to him for what he has so consistently done.' – Alan Sillitoe

'I have admired Peter Owen and his lone stand for years. He has published books that otherwise would not have been published. We owe a great deal to him and the few like him.' – Doris Lessing

'In these days of huge conglomerates in publishing, the survival of Peter Owen, a small, independent and adventurous imprint, is a cause for rejoicing. Like the French, the English literary world is a strangely provincial one. To mitigate this provincialism Peter Owen has done more than any other publisher in the post-war years. It has been through translations published by his firm that the English have been enabled to read the works of one of the world's greatest modern novelists, Shusaku Endo, and a host of other first-rate foreign writers.' – Francis King

'Admirers will wish the firm of Peter Owen many happy returns – including financial ones. We need them, if only to continue publishing the books richer publishers cannot afford.' – D.J. Enright

'Since 1968, my fiction has been published by Peter Owen, with the positive advantages of professional loyalty, personal friendship, meticulous editing and a practical belief that books are more than commercial commodities. I count myself fortunate.' – Peter Vansittart

'Peter Owen discovered me and published my first novel in 1987. Having been courted to descend into corporate publishing since then, I now realize the true value of this remarkable publisher and am returning to the fold. I am honoured and flattered to be alongside some of the most original novelists to have appeared anywhere. I salute you, Mr Owen, and thank you for your encouragement and for your proven excellence.' – Noel Virtue

'What I love about Peter Owen Publishers is the sense of freedom. First the pleasure of stepping into an attractive family house in a villagy street in Earl's Court rather than being confronted by hatchet-faced security men patrolling the concrete towers of some huge conglomerate. Then, business is conducted not in an anonymous office but in Peter's deliciously decadent study, complete with sofas, Persian rugs, pink cabbage-roses on the walls and bordello-pink paintwork. But these are frivolities compared with the all-important freedom he allows his authors. For fifty years this David amongst Goliaths has fought the cause of literature with incredible courage and Heaven on his side. Long may he prevail!' – Wendy Perriam

'By keeping alive that most difficult of all genres, the literary novel, Peter Owen has secured himself a place as one of the great independents and one of the outstanding publishers of the past half-century.'
– Jeremy Reed

'Of all the publishing men in my life Peter Owen has been the most constant, the most predictably unpredictable, the most infuriating, the one to whom I always come back.' – Margaret Crosland

'It is salutary for Peter Owen to have stayed independent amidst the predatory sea of global publishing, – in an age when the white whale of corporatism has steadily gulped up many an old and worthy house – and yet to have kept up the standards of taste, not just of world literature but of aesthetic production.' – Abdullah Hussein

'It's always marvellous to publish with Peter Owen. The speed and zest are unequalled. And his list is full of distinction and surprise!' – Barbara Hardy

'Over the years the list has been consistently a distinguished one.'
– Paul Bowles

'Congratulations on your list which has real quality.' – Graham Greene

'Dear Peter Owen – how much we owe you! I don't know any house which has taken on so many difficult books to sell and propagate. Blessings!' – Lawrence Durrell

'Peter Owen is an excellent discoverer of the hidden novels around the world and he encourages them to grow.' – Shusaku Endo

'Peter Owen was the only one who would have taken the risk of publishing the first book of an unknown writer in a remote country [*Cry, the Peacock*]. I marvelled at my luck in finding this small and highly original publishing house.' – Anita Desai

'Peter Owen is the prince of publishers. In an age of lightning turnovers for writers and shredding of books of merit, Mr Owen continues to uphold the great tradition of publishing works of quality and imagination and keeping those works in print in beautiful editions.' – James Purdy

'I congratulate you on all your successes and wish you many more in the years to come.' – Dame Moura Lympany

'Peter Owen is in a special category. By contrast with the large firms and their medium-sized dependants, he is that David whose successful and brilliant career has pioneered a new trend: the emergence of small publishing houses who look for opportunities in the face of the mammoth concerns.' – *Frankfurter Allgemeine Zeitung*

'Peter Owen already has the most intelligently selected list of foreign and experimental fiction. We owe him a great deal; he has made the novels of, among others, Asturias, Cendrars, Lengyel and the great Cora Sandel available here.'
– Martin Seymour-Smith, *Scotsman*

'Peter Owen has one of the most exotic lists in London publishing.' – *Sunday Telegraph*

'One of the most professional of British publishers . . . His knack of jumping on the right bandwagons has ensured that his books are always in demand . . . He has built up a formidable stable of authors.' – *Financial Times*

'A publishing impresario for whom books are global . . . We owe him the explosions not only of the only Catholic Japanese novelist, Shusaku Endo, but of Jane Bowles, James Purdy, Americans of shock genius and a host of translated Europeans, from Hermann Hesse to Chagall and Colette.' – David Hughes, *Mail on Sunday*

'The independent (some would say maverick) publisher Peter Owen is well known for his persistence in introducing foreign literature to the British public.' – *Publishers Weekly*

'Publishing is about the distribution of ideas. It is also an expanding business. It is important that it remains diverse and innovative. Peter Owen fits that bill.' – Clive Bradley, former Chief Executive, Publishers Association

'What is so remarkable about Peter Owen is that he has bucked every trend of dumbing down and continued to publish really worthwhile serious authors. Whether unknown or known, he has first spotted then not hesitated to invest his money and expertise in such writers. He is almost unique in this way.' – Martyn Goff

'My most vivid memory of my time at Peter Owen was of having lunch with John Lennon and Yoko Ono in a back room at Selfridges – Peter had published Ono's book *Grapefruit*, and they were there doing a signing – and of Peter leaning across the table into Lennon's face and saying, "I've had a few drinks and I'm going to be brutally frank . . ." What followed has vanished from my memory, but those inimitable words have stayed with me ever since. *Grapefruit* was in many ways a typical Peter Owen book: bold in concept, classically avant-garde and a marvellous

piece of opportunistic publishing. That Peter has survived, indeed thrived, continuing to publish such a list is, on the face of it, a marvel, but it owes everything to Peter's courage, his eye for an opportunity, his thrift, his ability to look for great books beyond these shores. Anyone who loves books owes him an enormous debt.' – Dan Franklin, Random House (former editor at Peter Owen)

'I am honoured to pay tribute to the great man. Peter Owen – easily mimicable but quite irreplaceable – has proved that it is possible to retain quality and independence without the hype and eventual trajectory to takeover – the place from which creative publishing has no return. There are plenty of excellent small publishers – they start up all the time – but whether, with the deadly power of retail conglomeration growing daily, the future Owens, with their distinctive lists, could now survive for five let alone fifty years is doubtful. But let us celebrate one who has. To wish a publisher many happy returns might carry the wrong message – but here's to the next Hesse.' – Philip Kogan, Kogan Page Publishers

'His encouragement of original writing is one of his great strengths, and in an era and publishing atmosphere where books are called "products" and those who select them "product managers", this is to be applauded. I congratulate him on his independence and stubborn individuality. A welcome spark, indeed.' – Jeremy Robson, Robson Books

'Many years ago, I came across a set of translations of the modern Italian writer Cesare Pavese in my local library; one by one, I read first the journals and then the novels, wondering vaguely who had made such a delightful writer available to an

English-speaking readership. The answer, of course, lay on the emphatic logo on the covers: Peter Owen, a name I came to associate with some of the most adventurous publishing in the United Kingdom over the last half-century, from Bowles to Endo, from Cocteau to de Chirico. Now, many years after my first encounter with Pavese and the house of Owen, I have the added pleasure of knowing its founder and presiding inspiration personally as a friend and lunch-time companion. So, Peter, a very happy fiftieth publishing birthday.'
– Robert Adkinson, Thames and Hudson

'As an independent publisher who has just celebrated his own fiftieth year of independence, I think I know better than most the qualities you need to survive at all as an independent, let alone for half a century, and Peter has them all in abundance. I have always recognized him as a major discoverer of literary talent, both in English and in translation, with a rare consistency of taste and standards, and he deserves the salute of his publishing colleagues.' – Ernest Hecht, Souvenir Press

'That Peter Owen has managed to survive as an independent publisher for the past fifty years is something of a miracle, not to say an example to all aspiring publishers. Large conglomerates have introduced unfair odds to the industry, with the result that literary merit and a fine tradition are being sacrificed in order to appease the faceless money gods. We desperately need the Peter Owens of this world to demonstrate that old-fashioned publishing, with its emphasis on excellence, is still alive and well. Long may it continue and flourish.' – Naim Attallah

'Dear Peter – All of us at City Lights, being in the same boat, congratulate you on navigating the adventurous waters of independent publishing all these years. Bravo!' – Lawrence Ferlinghetti, City Lights Books, San Francisco

'Apollinaire, Bowles, Cendrars, Dazai, Endo, Hesse, Laughlin [New Directions founder], Michaux, Miller, Mishima, Pasternak, Pound, Purdy, Sartre, Spark – one can find these names in both our catalogs, a sign that New Directions and Peter Owen are not just in the same field but in a special area of it. So it is with special enthusiasm from over here – across the Atlantic Ocean, that is – that we salute Peter Owen and congratulate him for his half-a-century history. Here's to many adventurous years ahead.' – Griselda Ohanessian, New Directions Publishers, New York

'Dear Peter – I don't want to be more of a hypocrite than is absolutely necessary, for, although I am delighted that your publishing house is still alive after fifty years, you and I have nonetheless had some basic differences of opinion. So, the best I can do for you is to say: I congratulate you on your fifty years of independence. Good luck.' – Roger Straus, Farrar, Straus and Giroux, New York

'Since the very beginning of his publishing career Peter Owen has shown a distinct and independent taste in literature. Cooperating with excellent advisers, he has been astute in his selection of books for translation from many countries, including Norway. Thank you, Peter, and congratulations on fifty years of distinguished and independent publishing.' – Eva Lie-Nielsen, Gyldendal Norsk Forlag, Oslo

Some Authors We Have Published

James Agee
Bella Akhmadulina
Tariq Ali
Kenneth Allsop
Alfred Andersch
Guillaume Apollinaire
Machado de Assis

Duke of Bedford
Oliver Bernard
Thomas Blackburn
Jane Bowles
Paul Bowles
Ilse, Countess von Bredow
Lenny Bruce

Finn Carling
Blaise Cendrars
Marc Chagall
Giorgio de Chirico
Uno Chiyo
Hugo Claus
Jean Cocteau
Albert Cohen
Colette
Richard Corson
Benedetto Croce
Margaret Crosland
e.e. cummings

Salvador Dalí
Osamu Dazai
Anita Desai
Fabián Dobles
William Donaldson

Autran Dourado
Lawrence Durrell

Isabelle Eberhardt
Sergei Eisenstein
Shusaku Endo
Erté

Knut Faldbakken
Ida Fink
Wolfgang Georg Fischer
Nicolas Freeling

Carlo Emilio Gadda
Rhea Galanaki
Salvador Garmendia
Michel Gauquelin
André Gide
Natalia Ginzburg
Jean Giono
Geoffrey Gorer
William Goyen
Julien Gracq
Sue Grafton
Robert Graves
Julien Green
George Grosz

Barbara Hardy
H.D.
Rayner Heppenstall
David Herbert
Gustaw Herling
Hermann Hesse
Shere Hite

Stewart Home
Abdullah Hussein
King Hussein of Jordan

Ruth Inglis
Grace Ingoldby
Yasushi Inoue

Hans Henny Jahnn
Karl Jaspers

Takeshi Kaiko
Anna Kavan
Yasunari Kawabata
Nikos Kazantzakis
Christer Kihlman
James Kirkup
Paul Klee

James Laughlin
Violette Leduc
József Lengyel
Robert Liddell
Francisco García Lorca
Moura Lympany

Dacia Maraini
Marcel Marceau
André Maurois
Henri Michaux
Henry Miller
Marga Minco
Yukio Mishima
Margaret Morris
Angus Wolfe Murray

Atle Næss
Gérard de Nerval
Anaïs Nin

Yoko Ono
Uri Orlev
Wendy Owen

Arto Paasilinna
Marco Pallis
Oscar Parland
Milorad Pavić
Boris Pasternak
Cesare Pavese
Octavio Paz
Mervyn Peake
Carlo Pedretti
Dame Margery Perham
Wendy Perriam
Edith Piaf
Fiona Pitt-Kethley
Ezra Pound
Marcel Proust
James Purdy

Graciliano Ramos
Jeremy Reed
Rodrigo Rey Rosa
Joseph Roth

Marquis de Sade
Cora Sandel
George Santayana
May Sarton
Jean-Paul Sartre
Ferdinand de Saussure
Gerald Scarfe
Albert Schweitzer

George Bernard Shaw
Isaac Bashevis Singer
Edith Sitwell
Susanne St Albans
Stevie Smith
C.P. Snow
Bengt Söderbergh
Vladimir Soloukhin
Natsume Sōseki
Muriel Spark
Gertrude Stein
Bram Stoker
August Strindberg

Rabindranath Tagore
Tambimuttu
Elisabeth Russell Taylor
Anne Tibble
Roland Topor

Anne Valery
Peter Vansittart
José J. Veiga
Tarjei Vesaas
Noel Virtue

Max Weber
Edith Wharton
William Carlos Williams
Phyllis Willmott
Monique Wittig

A.B. Yehoshua
Marguerite Young

Fakhar Zaman
Alexander Zinoviev